U0088123

語言是通往世界的橋梁

語言鳥 Parrot
語言是通往世界的橋梁

臨時急用！

會話 英語 生活

國際化脈動中，超實用的英語會話書！

Could you give

Ladies and gentlemen, welcome to our hotel, where you

Do you need any help?

I need some vegetables and

Many students like to stay at home

How about coming with u

It is a coincidence

基礎實用

語言鳥 **P**arrot

第一篇
哈啦最急用
JOINING IN THE CONVERSATION

第 1 章
打招呼
Chapter One Greeting

第 2 章
自我介紹
Chapter Two
Self-introduction

第 3 章

客套哈啦

Chapter Three Being
Polite and Being Social

第 4 章

請求與協助

Chapter Four
Asking For Help

第 5 章

交友

Chapter Five
Making Friends

第 6 章

狀況不佳時

Chapter Six
Feeling Poor

第 1 章

道別

Chapter Seven
Saying Goodbye

第 8 章

電話英文

Chapter Eight
Telephone English

第二篇
國外旅行最急用
IN TRAVELLING

第 1 章

問路

Chapter One
Asking for Directions

第 2 章

問時間

Chapter Two
Asking for Time

第 3 章

住宿英文

Chapter Three
Accommodation

第 4 章

購物

Chapter Four
Go Shopping

第 5 章

用餐

Chapter Five
Dining Out

第 6 章

機場

Chapter Six
In the Airport

哈啦最急用 Joining in the Conversation

第一章

臨時急用

打招呼
Chapter One Greeting

Unit ONE
早安/午安/晚安

 Track 1-1-01

Good morning.
早安
Good afternoon.
午安
Good evening.
晚安

與人見面,打招呼是簡單,直接,又必備的禮儀表示。無論正式或非正式場合,我們都可以根據當下的時間用早安、午安晚安與認識或者是陌生人打招呼。親切,簡單又不失禮。

急用會話

ADAM Hello.
您好!
MICHELLE Hello, good evening.
您好,晚安。
How are you?
您好嗎?
ADAM I am fine. Thank you.
我很好。謝謝您。

16

臨 時 用 語

1. 早安:
Good morning, Jeff!

Morning, Jeff!

Good morning to you.

Top of the morning!

2. 今天好:
Good day, sir!

Good day, madam!

單 字 解 說

1. morning 名詞:早晨
例 I went to school this morning.

我今早去上學。

2. afternoon 名詞:下午
例 Mary will go shopping this afternoon.

瑪莉今天下午會去購物。

3. evening 名詞:傍晚
例 My family usually takes a walk in the
evening.

我家人通常傍晚去散步。

Unit Two
你好嗎？（非正式）

Hi / Hello.
嗨！
What's up?
你好嗎?
How are you doing?
你好嗎?
Are you ok?
你好嗎?

除了在Unit One學習到的打招呼用語，當我們遇到年輕人，比較熟的朋友，或是比較輕鬆非正式的場合，本章介紹的What's up? (你好嗎? 近來如何?) 就可以用來打招呼問好。

急用會話

BILLY Hi! What's up, buddy?
嗨！你還好嗎，兄弟？
MARK Not much, and you?
還不賴，你呢？
BILLY Good.
我很好。

臨 時 用 語

1. 你好嗎:
What's happening?
What's going on?

2. 你近來如何:
How's life?
How's it going?
How's everything?

3. 兄弟,夥伴:
Buddy.
Pal.

單 字 解 說

1. **what** 疑問詞:什麼(東西、狀況)

例 What is that?
那個是什麼?

2. **how** 疑問詞:(東西、狀況)如何

例 How is today's weather?
今天天氣如何?

𝕌nit THREE

你好嗎?（正式）

How are you?
你好嗎?
How do you do?
你好?

在比較正式的場合如開會洽公，或是遇到初識的人，How are you?與How do you do?會比較適合用來當作初見面的招呼語，以表示禮貌。此外，第一章的Good morning，Good afternoon，以及Good evening也適用於正式場合作招呼語。要注意的是How do you do?的回答一樣是How do you do?，表示你好。

急用會話

FRANK How do you do?
你好?

MARY How do you do?
你好?

....

CANDY Hello, love. Long time no see. How are you?
嗨!好久不見?你好嗎?

JACK Good. How are you getting along?

20

很好啊。你過得如何呢？
CANDY Very well, thank you.
我很好。謝謝。

臨 時 用 語

1. 你好嗎?:

How are you getting along?
How's everything going with you?
How are things going with you?
How are things going?

單 字 解 說

1. get along 動詞：片語進展

例 How is Jennifer getting along with her
project?
珍妮佛的計畫進展如何？

2. good 形容詞：好、well 副詞：好

例 Irene is a good student.
艾琳是一個好學生。

例 You did very well!
你做得很好。

Unit FOUR

我很好。謝謝。那您呢?

Track 1-1-04

Very well, thank you. And you?
我很好。謝謝。那您呢?(正式)
Fine/Great!
我很好。(非正式)

當別人用How are you?或是What's up?這些疑問句來打招呼時,我們就要回覆這些招呼。基於禮貌,一般我們都會回答Good,Fine, Great,以正面的回應來繼續打招呼。除非是熟識的人,或是真的有狀況,我們才會回答當天真實的狀況。

急用會話

KATY Hello, Jack. How are you?
嗨!傑克,你好嗎?
JACK Very well, thank you. And you?
我很好。謝謝。那您呢?
KATY Very well, thank you.
我很好。謝謝。

臨 時 用 語

1. **我過得很好：**

I am pretty good.

I am doing great!

2. **我過得還可以：**

I am OK.

Not too bad.

3. **沒什麼事：**

Nothing much. / Nothing special.

So so.

4. **糟透了：**

It's terrible.

單 字 解 說

1. **pretty 副詞：非常**

例 The weather today is pretty nice.

今天天氣非常好。

2. **bad 形容詞：不好的；壞的**

例 Today's weather is bad.

今天天氣不好。

3. **terrible 形容詞：糟糕的**

例 Shrek looks terrible.

史瑞克看起來很糟。

Unit FIVE
嘿！你看起來不一樣了！

英文補給站

Track 1-1-05

Hi, you look different today!
嘿！你看起來不一樣了！
Are you Amy?
你是愛咪嗎？
Have we met before?
我們以前有見過嗎？

遇見面熟的人或是久未謀面的人，我們可以先用問對方Have we met before? (我們以前有見過嗎？)，來確認彼此是否認識以化解誤認人的尷尬，上列的三個句子也可以用於搭訕。

急用會話

HENRY Hi, you look different today!
嘿！你看起來不一樣了！
AMBER Sorry, but have we met before?
抱歉，但是我們以前有見過嗎？
I am Amber.
我是安珀。

臨 時 用 語

1. 你看起來很面熟:

You look familiar.

2. 我認識你嗎?:

Do I know you?

3. 你不記得我了嗎?:

Don't you remember me?

單 字 解 說

1. different 形容詞:不同的

例 Your red bag is very different from my
   blue one.

   你的紅包包跟我的藍包包很不一樣。

2. meet 動詞:遇見

(meet為不規則動詞三態變化:meet - met-met)

例 I met Jay in the restaurant this afternoon.

   我今天下午在餐廳遇見傑。

3. think 動詞:認為

(think為不規則的動詞三態變化:

think-thought-thought)

例 Mary thinks that her parents are partial
   to her brother.

   瑪莉認為她父母對弟弟偏心。

今天天氣不錯！

英文補給站

 Track 1-1-06

It is nice!
今天天氣不錯!
Today's weather is good, isn't it?
今天天氣不錯，可不是嗎?

除了一般的問候語可以用來化解初見面的尷尬氣氛之外，談論天氣也是許多英美人士常用於初見面破冰或搭訕的方式。所以，回答時，基本上都會給予肯定的回覆。

急用會話

JAMES Today's weather is good, isn't it?
今天天氣不錯，可不是嗎?

JOYCE Indeed! It couldn't be better!
的確!它好到不能再好了!

JAMES Hello, I am James.
嗨，我是詹姆士。

JOYCE Nice to meet you. I am Joyce.
很高興認識你，我是喬伊斯。

臨 時 用 語

1. 今天天氣不錯:
It is fair.

Today's weather is good.

It is sunny.

2. 今天雨下得好大：

It rains a lot.

It is rainy.

3. 很高興認識你：

Glad to meet you.

I am happy to know you.

It is nice to know you.

單 字 解 說

1. **weather 名詞：天氣**

例 The weather in spring is usually pleasant.

春天的天氣通常是宜人的。

2. **better 形容詞：更好的（good的比較級）**

例 Are you feeling better?

你感覺比較好一點了嗎？

3. **fair 形容詞：美好的；晴朗的**

例 The weather in the southern Taiwan is often fair.

台灣南部天氣通常晴朗。

4. **rain 動詞：下雨**

例 It rains a lot in Yi-lan.

宜蘭常下雨。

Unit SEVEN
好久不見了！

Track 1-1-07

Long time no see.
好久不見了！
What's new?
近來有什麼新消息嗎？
Good to see you again.
很高興又再見到你。

遇到久未謀面的朋友，我們可以用What's new?
(近來有什麼新消息嗎?)來打招呼跟問候近況。
須注意Long time no see原本就是從中文「好久
不見」直譯，而演變成今日通用的問候語，是
非常口語的用法，不適用於正式場合。

急用會話

FAY Is that you, Steven? Long time no see!
史蒂夫是你嗎?好久不見!
STEVEN Hey, Fay. Long time no see!
How are you?
嘿!費。好久不見!你好嗎?
FAY I am fine, thank you. What's new?
我很好，謝謝。有什麼新消息嗎?

28

臨 時 用 語

1. **好久不見：**
It's been so long.
It's been such a long time.

2. **我很高興再見到你：**
Nice to meet you again.

3. **沒什麼：**
Nothing special.
Same as usual.

單 字 解 說

1. **that 代名詞：那個**
例 I want that.
我要那個。

2. **long 形容詞：(時間)長的**
例 Sean spent long hours finishing his home-work.
尚恩花了長時間完成他的作業。

3. **time 名詞：時間**
例 Time is money.
時間就是金錢。

Unit EIGHT
歡迎!

Track 1-1-08

Welcome!
歡迎!
Welcome. Come on in!
歡迎光臨!
You are very welcome.
歡迎!

當遇到生意場合,要迎接嘉賓或是客人時,一句Welcome就可以正式的問候並迎接客人。當客人要離開時,一句Welcome to come again.就可以不失禮地問候並且與客人道別。

急用會話

SIMON Ladies and gentlemen, welcome to our hotel, where you will get high-level enjoyment.
各位女士先生,歡迎來到我們飯店。在這裡你會享受到高級的服務。
Please enjoy yourselves here and feel at home.
請盡興且把這裡當成自己的家。

臨 時 用 語

1. 歡迎到我家：

Welcome to my house.

Welcome to my place.

2. 不用客氣：

Make yourself at home.

Make yourself comfortable.

Be my guest.

Help yourself.

單 字 解 說

1. come 動詞：來

例 Jason finally came home from his office.

傑森終於從公司回到家了。

2. hotel 名詞：旅館

例 They stayed in a hotel rather than a B&B.

他們待在一間旅館而非民宿。

3. home 名詞：家

例 Many students like to stay at home and
play video games.

很多學生喜歡待在家玩電動。

Unit NINE
真巧!

 Track 1-1-09

What a coincidence!
真巧
What a lovely surprise to meet you here!
真巧遇到你!

在路上不期而遇認識的友人,可以用What a coincidence! (真巧)來問候跟表達驚喜之情。

急用會話

EARL Hey, my friend. It's been a while.
嘿,我的朋友,好久不見了。

IRENE Hi, Earl. What a coincidence!
嗨,厄爾。真巧!

EARL Yeah, how have you been?
是啊,你好嗎?

IRENE I've been good. Thank you. How are you?
還不錯啊,謝謝。你呢?

EARL Same as usual.
老樣子啦。

臨 時 用 語

1. 真巧遇見你:

What a lovely coincidence running into you!

Imagine meeting you here!

It is a small world!

What a small world!

單 字 解 說

1. coincidence 名詞:湊巧,巧合

例 It is a coincidence that my birthday is the same as hers.

我跟她的生日同一天純屬巧合。

2. lovely 形容詞:討人喜愛的

例 What a lovely day it is!

今天多美好啊!

3. surprise 名詞:驚喜

例 The present is quite a surprise to my father.

這個禮物對我爸是個驚喜。

4. small 形容詞:小的

例 Jack has a small car.

傑克有一台小車。

NOTE BOOK

哈啦最急用 Joining in the Conversation

第二章

時用
臨急

自我介紹
Chapter Two Self-introduction

Unit ONE
你怎麼稱呼?

 Track 1-2-01

What is your name?
你怎麼稱呼?
My name is Jean.
我名字叫做珍。
You can call me John.
你可以叫我約翰。

自我介紹時,一定是先從自己的姓名(name)介紹開始;同樣的,想要認識一個人的時候,也可以先從詢問如何稱呼開始,以表示禮貌。

急用會話

JOHN Hey, what is your name?
嘿,你怎麼稱呼?
JEAN My name is Jean. You are?
我叫做珍。你是?
JOHN You can call me John.
你可以叫我約翰。
Nice to meet you, Jean.
很高興認識你,珍。

臨 時 用 語

1. 你叫什麼名字?:

May I have your name?

Your name, please?

Name, please?

2. 我叫佩姬:

Peggy.

I am Peggy.

Please call me Peggy.

單 字 解 說

1. name 名詞：名字

例 The dog's name is Lucky.

這隻狗的名字叫來福。

2. nice 形容詞：好的

例 Mrs. Smith is a nice teacher.

史密斯太太是一個好老師。

3. please 動詞：請

例 Please sit down.

請坐下。

Unit Two
你從哪裡來?

 Track 1-2-02

Where are you from?
你從哪裡來?
What is your nationality?
你是哪一國人?
I am from Seoul.
我來自首爾。
I am a Korean.
我是一個韓國人。

自我介紹時,可以說明自己是從哪裡來,讓
對方可以更了解你。我們可以詢問對方國籍
(nationality),藉由他的回答,繼續聊天的話
題。

急用會話

LILY Glad to meet you. I am Lily.
很高興認識你。我是莉莉。
I am from Seoul. Where are you from?
我來自首爾。你是從哪來?
STEVE I am from America. Nice to meet
you.
我來自美國。很高興認識你。
What is your nationality?

你是哪國人?
LILY I am a Korean.
我是韓國人。

臨 時 用 語

1. 你從哪裡來?:
Where do you come from?

2. 我從＿＿＿來:
I come from ＿＿＿.

3. 國家與國籍
中國: China 中國人: Chinese
台灣: Taiwan 台灣人: Taiwanese
美國: U.S.A. 美國人: American
英國: U.K. 英國人: British
法國: France 法國人: French
德國: Germany 德國人: German
西班牙: Spain 西班牙人: Spanish
希臘: Greece 希臘人: Greek
荷蘭: Holland 荷蘭人: Dutch
日本: Japan 日本人: Japanese
韓國: Korea 韓國人: Korean
印度: India 印度人: Indian
澳洲: Australia 澳洲人: Australian

Unit THREE

你是從事何種工作?

Track 1-2-03

What do you do?
你是從事何種工作?
What's your job?
你是做什麼的?
I am a secretary.
我是一個秘書。
I work for a computer company.
我在一間電腦公司上班。

自我介紹時,可以介紹自己的職業讓對方更瞭解你。然而,若要詢問對方職業(occupation)時,因為這是屬於比較個人領域的問題,所以務必要注意禮貌。

急用會話

DAVID Olivia, long time no see! What do you do?
奧莉薇亞,好久不見!你是從事何種工作?
OLIVIA I am a secretary and I work for a computer company.
我是一個秘書,我在一間電腦公司上班。
What's your job?
你是做什麼的?

> **DAVID** I am a salesperson now.
> 我現在是個業務。

臨 時 用 語

1. 你是什麼職業?:
Who are you?

Where do you work?

What's your occupation?

2. 我是_____。:
I am a _____.

I work as a _____.

3. 常見職業名稱:
採購員:buyer　業務員:clerk

農夫:farmer　警衛:guard

記者:reporter　警察:police-officer

辦公人員:officer　律師:lawyer

藥劑師:pharmacist

家庭主婦:housekeeper　廚師:cook

秘書:secretary　技術人員:technician

舞者:dancer　漫畫家:cartoonist

畫家:painter　美容師:cosmetologist

美髮師:hairdresser　設計師:designer

藝術家:artist　駕駛人:driver

電匠:electrician　水管工:plumber

Unit FOUR

你電話幾號?

Track 1-2-04

What is your phone number?

你電話幾號?

My phone number is _____.

我的電話號碼是_____.

Is your phone number _____?

你的電話號碼是_____?

如果要跟對方保持聯繫時,提供自己的電話號碼或詢問對方的電話號碼(telephone number),是一個不錯的方式。

SAM Jack, do you have a cell phone?

傑克,你有手機嗎?

JACK Yes. What's up?

有啊,怎麼了?

SAM What is your phone number?

你電話幾號?

JACK My phone number is 0915-466-725.

我電話號碼是0915-466-725。

SAM Thanks!

多謝!

42

臨 時 用 語

數字英文

0: zero 1: one 2: two 3: three 4: four
5. five 6: six 7: seven 8: eight 9: nine
10: ten

字 解 說

1. telephone 名詞：電話

例 I just talked to a client on the telephone.

我剛跟客戶講電話。

2. cell phone 名詞：手機

例 May I use your cell phone?

我可以借用你的手機嗎?

(雖然中文我們說: 我可以跟你 "借" 手機嗎?，
然而，在英文裡，我們用的動詞是use(使用)，
而非borrow(借)喔。)

3. number 名詞：號碼

例 Jamie's door number is 35.

傑米的門牌號碼是35。

你住在哪裡?

英文補給站 Track 1-2-05

Where do you live?
你住在哪裡?
What is your address?
你的地址是什麼?
I live in Taipei.
我住在台北。

跟比較熟識的朋友或是商辦場合，我們可以
提供自己的住所或公司地址(address)給對方知
道，或是詢問對方聯絡地址，保持聯繫。

急用會話

MARIE Do you live around here?
你住附近嗎?
CLARK No.
不是。
MARIE Where do you live?
你住在哪裡?
CLARK I live in Taipei.
我住在台北。

臨 時 用 語

1. 你住在哪裡?:

May I have your address?

Address, please?

2. 我的地址是 _____.:

My address is _____.

3. 地址英譯:

常常為地址不知如何用英文表示而苦惱嗎?台
灣郵政提供中文地址英譯服務,只要到下列網
頁,填上中文地址,就可以迅速知道英文地
址如何說跟寫了喔。台灣郵政中文地址英譯網
站:http://www.post.gov.tw/post/index.jsp

單 字 解 說

1. live 動詞:居住

例 A lot of people love to live in the country.

很多人喜歡住在鄉下。

2. address 名詞:地址

例 Please write down your home address
here.

請你在這裡寫上你家地址。

Unit SIX

你什麼時候出生的?

 Track 1-2-06

When were you born?

你什麼時候出生的?

What date is your birthday?

你生日幾號?

生日(birthday)都是屬於比較個人領域的問題,所以在詢問時務必要注意禮貌。通常我們都是跟比較熟悉的朋友詢問這一個問題。

急用會話

BETTY Zoe, when were you born?

柔伊,你是何時出生的?

ZOE I was born on August third, 1968.

我出生於1968年8月3日。

BETTY You look younger than your age.

你看起來比實際年齡年輕。

ZOE Thank you.

謝謝。

臨 時 用 語

月份英文

1月：January 2月：February

3月：March 4月：April

5月：May 6月：June 7月：July

8月：August 9月：September

10月：October 11月：November

12月：December

單 字 解 說

1. birthday 名詞：生日

例 Happy birthday to you.

祝你生日快樂。

2. date 名詞：日期

例 I forget the date for the party.

我忘了宴會的日期了。

3. bear 動詞：生

(bear為不規則動詞三態變化:bear-bore-born)

例 A baby was born this morning.

今天早上一個嬰兒生出來了。

Unit SEVEN

你幾歲？

 Track 1-2-07

How old are you?

你幾歲？

I am thirty five years old.

我是三十五歲。

年齡(age)都是屬於比較個人領域的問題，所以在詢問時務必要注意禮貌。通常我們都是跟比較熟悉的朋友詢問這一個問題。

急用會話

HENRY Vivian, how old are you?

薇薇安，你幾歲了？

VIVIAN I am thirty five years old.

我三十五歲。

HENRY Really! You look younger than your age!

真的！你看起來比你實際年齡年輕。

VIVIAN Thank you.

謝謝。

臨 時 用 語

1. 你幾歲?:

What is your age?

How old?

2. 我26歲:

Twenty six.

I am twenty six.

I am twenty six years of age.

3. 他跟我同歲:

He is my age.

單 字 解 說

1. old 形容詞：老的

例 My mother is getting old.

我媽媽漸漸地變老。

2. age 名詞：年齡

例 When I was your age, I worked very hard.

當我在你這個年紀的時候，我很認真工作。

你的星座/生肖是?

 Track 1-2-08

What is your star sign?

你的星座是?

What is your Chinese star sign?

你的生肖是?

I am an Aries.

我是牡羊座。

My sign is a money.

我生肖屬猴。

聊天時,在西方文化中,可以問對方星座(star sign)或者是介紹東方生肖(Chinese star sign),增加趣味性。要注意的是,雖然在台灣或日本,血型(blood type)也是一個有趣的話題,但外國人覺得血型是比較個人隱私的事,所以剛認識時,建議不要詢問對方血型喔。

急用會話

ADAM Winnie, what is your star sign?

溫妮,你的星座是什麼?

WINNIE I am an Aries because I was born on April fourth.

我是牡羊座,因為我生日是四月四號。

ADAM What is your Chinese star sign?

你的生肖是什麼?

WINNIE My sign is a monkey because I was born in 1979.

我屬猴,因為我生於1979年。

臨 時 用 語

1. **12星座的英文寫法:**

   白羊座: Aries　金牛座: Taurus

   雙子座: Gemini　巨蟹座: Cancer

   獅子座: Leo　處女座: Virgo

   天秤座: Libra　天蠍座: Scorpio

   射手座: Sagittarius　摩羯座: Capricorn

   水瓶座: Aquarius　雙魚座: Pisces

2. **12生肖的英文說法:**

   鼠: Rat　牛: Ox　虎: Tiger

   兔: Rabbit　龍: Dragon　蛇: Snake

   馬: Horse　羊: Goat　猴: Monkey

   雞: Rooster　狗: Dog　豬: Pig

Unit NINE

你喜歡吃什麼?

 Track 1-2-09

What do you like to eat?
你喜歡吃什麼?
What is your favorite food?
你最喜歡的食物什麼?
I like to eat chocolate.
我喜歡吃巧克力。

聊天問答中,可以問對方What do you like to eat? (你喜歡吃什麼?),藉由知道對方的喜好的食物,可以更了解對方,也可以keep the ball rolling,讓對話更豐富有趣地進行下去喔。

急用會話

TERA Smith, what do you like to eat?
史密斯,你喜歡吃什麼?

BEN I like to eat chocolate because it is sweet.
我喜歡吃巧克力,因為它很甜。

What is your favorite food?
你最喜歡的食物什麼?

TERA My favorite food is chips.
我最喜歡的食物是薯片。

臨 時 用 語

零食英文：

零食: snack　葡萄乾: raisin
棒棒糖: lollipop　什錦堅果: mixed nuts
爆米花: popcorn　霜淇淋: ice cream
果凍: jelly　開心果: pistachio nut
餅乾: cookie　布丁: pudding
糖果: candy

單 字 解 說

1. eat 動詞：吃

   例 Lary did not eat breakfast.
   賴瑞沒有吃早餐。

2. favorite 形容詞：最喜愛的

   例 My favorite movie is Twilight.
   我最喜歡的電影是暮光之城。

3. food 名詞：食物

   例 Ants preserve food for winter.
   螞蟻儲存食物以過冬。

4. because 連接詞：因為

   例 I eat so much because I am hungry.
   我吃那麼多是因為我餓了。

Unit TEN

你的嗜好是什麼？

 Track 1-2-10

What are your hobbies?

你的嗜好是什麼？

My hobby is listening to music.

我嗜好是聽音樂。

What kind of music do you like?

你喜歡什麼樣的音樂？

聊天中，可以問對方What are your hobbies? (你的嗜好是什麼?)，詢問對方的嗜好，添加話題的趣味性，也可以更了解對方的品味。

急用會話

EVE Ben, what are your hobbies?

班，你的嗜好是什麼？

BEN My hobby is listening to music.

我嗜好是聽音樂。

EVEN What kind of music do you like?

你喜歡什麼樣的音樂？

BEN I like pop music. And you?

我喜歡流行樂，你呢？

臨 時 用 語

1. 你的興趣是什麼?:
What are your interests?

2. 你有空時都做什麼?:
What do you do in your free time?

3. 你喜歡聽音樂嗎?:
Do you enjoy listening to music?

4. 音樂英文:

古典音樂 classical music

流行音樂 pop music

重金屬音樂 heavy metal

搖滾樂 Rock'n Roll

電子樂 electronic music

爵士樂 Jazz

藍調 blues

說唱 Rap

嘻哈 Hip-Hop

民俗音樂 Folk

舞曲 Dance

迪斯可 Disco

音樂劇 Musical

歌劇 Opera

能不能給我一張名片?

英文補給站

 Track 1-2-11

Could I have your business card?

能不能給我一張名片?

Do you want to exchange numbers?

你要交換電話嗎?

在正式一點的社交場合,或商業場合,交換名片(business card)是件很重要的事。在一般朋友的社交場合,想要跟認識的朋友在更進一步聯繫,就可以跟對方交換電話或其他的通訊方式。

急用會話

GEORGE Hello, Eddy, this is Lance, my colleague.

嗨,艾迪,這是我同事蘭斯。

And Lance, this is Eddy, my classmate in college.

蘭斯,這是我大學同學艾迪。

EDDY Nice to meet you, Lance. Could I have your business card?

跟高興見到你,蘭斯。能不能給我一張名片?

LANCE Nice to meet you and this is my

card.
跟高興見到你，這是我的名片。

臨 時 用 語

1. 能不能給你你的名片呢?:

Your business card, please.

2. 這是我的名片:

Here is my card.

3. 能不能給我你的電郵?:

Could I have your email address?

4. 能不能給我你的Facebook帳號?:

May I have your Facebook account?

單 字 解 說

1. business 名詞：生意，商業

例 How is your business?

你最近生意如何?

2. card 名詞：卡片；名片

例 Here is my card.

這是我的名片。

3. exchange 動詞：交換

例 I want to exchange some NT dollars for

dollars.

我想把一些台幣換成美金。

這是你的狗嗎?

英文補給站

 Track 1-2-12

Is this your dog?

這是你的狗嗎?

Do you have a pet?

你養寵物嗎?

Are you a dog-person or a cat-person?

你比較喜歡狗還是貓?

外國很喜歡聊Are you a dog-person or a cat-person? (你比較喜歡狗還是貓?)。所以,第一次見面,如果找不到話題聊天,聊聊彼此的寵物或者是喜歡的動物也可以做為了解彼此的開始。

急用會話

JUDY That's a cute puppy.

這真是一隻可愛的小狗。

Is that your dog?

這是你的狗嗎?

JANE Yes, its name is Lucky. Do you have a pet, too?

是啊,它叫做來福。你也養寵物嗎?

JUDY No. My house is too small.

沒有。我家太小了。

臨 時 用 語

1. 寵物英文:

   狗 dog　　貓 cat　　小狗 puppy

   小貓 kitty　魚 fish　鯉魚 carp

   鳥 bird　鸚鵡 parrot　鴿子 dove

2. 流浪狗:

   stray dog

3. 流浪貓:

   stray cat

4. 我真希望我能養寵物:

   I wish I could keep pets.

5. 他很喜歡動物:

   He likes animals so much.

單 字 解 說

1. pet 名詞:寵物

   例 Kathy keeps many pets.

   凱西養了很多寵物。

Unit THIRTEEN
我身材中等

Track 1-2-13

I am of medium height and build.

我身材中等。

I am 167 centimeters tall.

我167公分高。

I weigh 60 kilograms.

我60公斤重。

身高體重身材比較不會是第一次聊天的話題，
但是去到國外，我們仍是要懂得如何描述自
己的身高(height)和體重(weight)，以備不時之
需。

NURSE How tall are you?

你多高？

PATIENT I am 167 centimeters tall.

我167公分高。

NURSE How much do you weigh?

你多重？

PATIENT I weigh 60 kilograms.

我60公斤重。

臨 時 用 語

1. 我身材中等：

I am medium-height.

I am an average-sized woman.

2. 我身材嬌小：

I am petite.

I am small.

3. 我身材肥胖：

I am overweight.

單 字 解 說

1. high 形容詞：高的

例 The mountain is high.

這山真高。

2. weigh 動詞：重

例 The giant baby weighs 4,000 grams.

這個巨嬰重四千公克。

NOTE BOOK

哈啦最急用 Joining in the Conversation

第三章

臨時 | 時用
急用

客套哈啦
Chapter Three Being Polite and Being Social

Unit ONE
謝謝

 Track 1-3-01

Thank you.
謝謝你。

Cheers.
謝謝。

Thank you for your help.
謝謝的你的幫忙。

Thank you. (謝謝你)是再常用也不過的一句道謝語。表示感謝別人的幫助，邀約等等，無論任何場合，可以用thanks 表示感謝。唯須注意cheers來自於英國口語用法，是非常非正式的口語用法，僅適用於熟識的朋友。

急用會話

JIM It's so cold.
好冷喔。

Can you close the window for me, please?
可以請你幫我關一下窗戶嗎？

MAY Yes.
好啊。

JIM Thank you for your help.
謝謝你的幫忙。

64

臨 時 用 語

1. 真是感謝:

Thanks a lot.

Many thanks.

Thank you very much.

I really appreciate that.

2. 感謝你的邀請:

Thanks for your invitation.

單 字 解 說

1. thank 動詞:謝謝

例 Jim thanked his brother for help.

吉姆謝謝他哥哥的幫忙。

名詞:謝謝

例 Thanks a million!

萬分感謝。

2. help 動詞:幫助

例 Could you help me with the assignments?

你幫我處理這些作業好嗎?

名詞:幫助

例 The dictionary has been a great help.

字典幫了大忙。

$\mathcal{Unit}$ TWO
不用客氣

 Track 1-3-02

You are welcome!
不用客氣。
Not at all.
不用客氣。
No worries.
不用客氣(非正式)。

當有人對你說Thank you時,你可以回答You are welcome! (不用客氣)來表示禮貌。而No worry 適用於熟識朋友之間。

急用會話

VINCENT Thank you for your present.
謝謝你的禮物。
It's lovely.
它很棒。
IRIS You are welcome!
不用客氣。
I hope you will like it.
我希望你會喜歡它。

臨 時 用 語

1. 不客氣：

Not a problem.

2. 小事一樁：

Not a big deal.

3. 我的榮幸：

My pleasure.

單 字 解 說

1. **present** 名詞：禮物

例 Children like to receive presents at Christmas.

在聖誕節，小孩子喜歡收到禮物。

2. **lovely** 形容詞：好的；可愛的

例 You look lovely in red.

你穿紅的很可愛。

3. **hope** 動詞：希望

例 Many parents hope that their children will have a bright future.

很多家長希望自己的小孩會有一個不錯的未來。

Unit THREE

道歉

英文補給站

Track 1-3-03

Sorry.

抱歉。

Excuse me.

不好意思。

Pardon.

不好意思。

I am sorry for my mistake.

我對我的錯誤道歉。

Sorry是比較正式的用法，表示對一件事感到遺憾或抱歉；Excuse me跟Pardon比較適用於一般遇到陌生人或發生小意外時用。

急用會話

WILLIAM Wow, you hurt me!

哇，你弄痛我了。

STACY I am very sorry about it.

我很抱歉。

WILLIAM Never mind.

算了。

68

臨 時 用 語

1. 我很抱歉弄傷你：

I am sorry to hurt you.

I am sorry for hurting you.

2. 這是我的錯：

It is my fault.

3. 我道歉：

I apologize.

I beg your pardon.

單 字 解 說

1. sorry 形容詞：感到抱歉的；感到遺憾的

例 I am sorry for being late for the meeting.

抱歉我開會遲到。

2. mistake 名詞：錯誤

例 People make mistakes sometimes.

人有時會犯錯。

3. fault 名詞：錯誤；缺失

例 Every man has his faults.

人非聖賢，孰能無過。

𝕌nit FOUR
沒關係

Track 1-3-04

It's all right.
沒關係。
It's OK.
沒關係。
Never mind.
算了。

當有人跟你說Sorry時, 你可以回答It's all right. (沒關係)來表達對於對方歉意的原諒與不介意。

急用會話

TOM I am really sorry for breaking your watch.
我很抱歉打破你的花瓶。
I didn't mean it.
我不是故意的。
Please forgive me.
請原諒我。
SANDRA It's all right.
沒關係。

臨 時 用 語

1. 沒關係：

That's alright.

It doesn't matter.

Forget it.

You are fine.

Don't be sorry.

單 字 解 說

1. never 副詞：絕不

例 I have never smoked before.

我從未抽過菸。

2. matter 動詞：重要；有關係

例 Your attitude matters.

你的態度很重要。

3. forgive 動詞：原諒

(forgive為不規則三態變化forgive-forgave-forgiven)

例 To err is human; to forgive divine.

人難免錯誤;寬恕別人是神聖的。

Unit FIVE
是啊！/好啊！

Track 1-3-05

Yes.
是啊。
Yep.
是啊。
Sure.
好啊。
OK.
好啊。

本單元介紹的詞可用於口語上表達「肯定」或「當然」的語氣。

急用會話

RACHAEL Don't you think it is cold here?
你不覺得這裡很冷嗎？
RANDOLPH Yep.
是啊。
RACHAEL Would you like to have a cup of coffee?
你要一杯咖啡嗎？
RANDOLPH Sure.
好啊。

臨 時 用 語

1. 好，麻煩你：

Yes, please.

2. 好：

I'd love to.

Why not?

單 字 解 說

1. **sure** 副詞

例 It's sure freezing cold outside.

外面實在很冷。

2. **love** 動詞：喜愛

例 Mandy loves diamonds.

曼蒂喜歡鑽石。

3. **why** 疑問詞：為什麼

例 Why do you go to school on Sunday?

你為什麼星期天去上學？

Unit SIX

我瞭解了

Track 1-3-06

Do you get it?
你瞭解了嗎?
I get your point.
我瞭解了。

當我們了解別人說話的意思,或是掌握到他意思的重點,我們可以說I get your point. (我瞭解了)。

急用會話

ALLEN I caught a cold.
我感冒了。
NEAL You should drink more water and exercise more.
你應該要多喝水跟多運動。
Do you get it?
你瞭解了嗎?
ALLEN I get your point.
我瞭解了。
You mean I should take good care of myself.
你是說我要好好照顧自己。

臨 時 用 語

1. 你懂嗎?:

See?

Can't you see?

Do you understand?

2. 我懂了:

I see.

I understand.

I got you.

單 字 解 說

1. get 動詞：得到；理解

(get為不規則三態變化: get-got-gotten)

例 Please don't get me wrong.

請不要誤解我的意思。

2. see 動詞：看到；了解

例 It's hard to see what my boss means.

我很難瞭解老闆的意思。

Unit SEVEN
恭喜恭喜!

 Track 1-3-07

Congratulations!
恭喜恭喜!
I am glad to hear that.
我很高興聽到這個消息。
Good for you.
這對你來說很好。

當朋友親人有好事降臨或喜事發生,我們可以
說Congratulations! (恭喜恭喜!)來表示恭賀或祝
賀之意。

急用會話

DENNY Tim, long time no see. How are you?
提姆,好久不見了。你好嗎?
TIM Great! Guess what? I just got a promotion!
很好啊!你知道嗎?我剛升職了!
DENNY Congratulations!
恭喜恭喜!
TIM Thank you.
謝謝。

臨 時 用 語

1. 我真是為你高興:

I am really happy for you.

2. 那真是個好消息:

That's really good news.

單 字 解 說

1. hear 動詞:聽見

例 You can hear birds chirping in a forest.

你可以在森林裡聽見小鳥叫。

2. guess 動詞:猜測

例 The magician can guess what will happen next.

那個魔術師能推測出接下來會發生什麼事。

3. promotion 名詞:升職

例 I must congratulate you on your promotion.

恭喜你升職了。

4. news 名詞:消息;新聞

例 I have a piece of good news for you.

我有一個好消息要跟你說。

Unit Eight
真是令人難以置信

I cannot believe it.
我真是不敢相信。
It's unbelievable.
這真是令人難以置信。
Marvellous!
真是令人難以置信。

本單元介紹的句子可用來表示對一件好事感到「驚喜」或「驚訝」之情。

急用會話

GRAM Guess what!
你知道嗎?
My girlfriend, Miranda, is going to marry me tomorrow!
我女朋友米蘭達明天就要嫁給我了!
HEATHER Really?
真的嗎?
I cannot believe it.
我真是不敢相信。

78

臨時用語

1. 這是真的嗎?:

It can't be.

Really?

2. 真是令人難以置信:

It's incredible.

3. 真是太棒了:

Just wonderful.

單字解說

1. believe 動詞:相信

例 That kid believes every word his mother says.

那個小孩相信她媽媽說的每一句話。

2. marvelous 形容詞:令人驚嘆的;驚奇的

例 Albert has a marvellous gift for music.

亞伯特有音樂方面的非凡天賦。

3. incredible 形容詞:不可置信的

例 The show is really incredible.

這個表演真是令人難以置信。

℧nit NINE
做得好！

英文補給站

 Track 1-3-09

Well-done!
做得好！

You are doing well!
你表現得很好！

Good job!
做得好！

當小朋友或同事表現出色時，我們可以藉由說
一句Well-done! (做得好) 來鼓勵他們或讚賞他們
的表現。

急用會話

NELSON Hey, Dean. You look great!
嘿，汀。你看起來不錯喔！

How is everything?
怎麼了？

DEAN I just closed a one-million dollar
project.
我剛做完一個一百萬的案子。

NELSON Good job!
做得好！

臨 時 用 語

1. 做得好：

You did a great job.

Cool.

Good.

Excellent.

單 字 解 說

1. million 名詞：百萬

例 She has five million dollars.

她有五百萬元。

2. project 名詞：方案

例 It takes two months to finish this project.

完成這個案子需要兩個月。

3. excellent 形容詞：極佳的

例 Emily gets a nice job because she is excel-

lent in English.

艾蜜莉得到了一個好工作，因為她英文

極佳。

$\mathcal{U}$nit TEN
我也這麼認為

 Track 1-3-10

I think so, too.
我也這麼認為。
Me, too.
我也是。
I don't think so.
我不這麼認為。

I think so, too. (我也這麼認為)等本單元介紹的
句子可用於表達自己對事物或他人意見的同意
或贊同與否。

急用會話

JASMINE It's late. How will you go
home?
很晚了。你要怎麼回家?

TRACY I do not know. There is no bus
stop around.
我不知道。這附近沒有站牌。

JASMINE I will drive Jenny home. Do
you need a ride?
我會開車載珍妮回家,你呢?

TRACY I think so, too.
我想我也需要。

82

1. 我也是(表示贊同)：

Anything you say!

I agree with you.

Sounds alright to me.

Okay, let's.

單 字 解 說

1. **late** 形容詞：晚的

例 Because of the traffic jam, Berry arrived home in the late afternoon.

因為塞車，貝瑞下午很晚才回到家。

2. **drive** 動詞：駕駛；開車

例 Edward doesn't know how to drive.

愛德華不知道怎麼開車。

3. **agree** 動詞：同意

例 Many parents don't agree with their children on many things.

許多家長和孩子在許多事情上意見不一致。

Unit ELEVEN
當然!

 Track 1-3-11

Of course!
當然!
Definitely!
當然!
Of course not!
當然不!

本單元介紹的句子適用於表達自己對事物或他人意見的同意與否以及自身所抱持的「堅決」態度。

急用會話

RUTH Excuse me. May I use your cell phone?
不好意思。我可以借用你的手機嗎?
JASON Why? What happened?
為什麼?怎麼了?
RUTH I just lost mine. Could I use yours?
我剛掉了我的。我可以借用你的嗎?
JASON Of course.
當然。

臨 時 用 語

1. 當然：
Certainly.
Absolutely.
You can say that again.

2. 絕不：
No way!
Not a chance!

單 字 解 說

1. **definitely 副詞：當然；一定**
例 Lorry always keeps his word so he is definitely coming.
   勞瑞總是遵守承諾，所以他一定會來的。

2. **certainly 副詞：當然；一定**
例 They will certainly make it because they work hard.
   他們那麼努力一定會成功。

3. **absolutely 副詞：絕對地、完全地**
例 The cake is absolutely delicious.
   那蛋糕絕對好吃。

Unit TWELVE
振作！

英文補給站

 Track 1-3-12

Cheer up!
振作！
Calm down.
冷靜。
I am with you.
我會支持你。

本單元介紹的句子適用於鼓勵人們，支持友人振作。

急用會話

TINA Hi, Joseph. You look terrible.
嗨，約瑟夫。你看起來很糟。
Are you OK?
你還好嗎？
JOSEPH I feel very bad. I was just fired.
我感覺很糟。我剛被解雇了。
TINA I am sorry to hear that.
我很遺憾聽到這個消息。
Cheer up!
振作！

86

臨 時 用 語

1. 放輕鬆點：
Take it easy.
Relax.

2. 不要低估你自己：
Don't underestimate yourself.

單 字 解 說

1. cheer 動詞：使振奮；鼓舞

例 The inspiring story cheered the little boy.
這一個勵志的故事鼓舞了這個小男孩。

2. easy 形容詞：從容的；放鬆的

例 She is good at speaking so she is easy in
conversation.
她擅長說話所以她與人交談時很從容。

3. relax 動詞：放鬆

例 Listening to soft music can relax your
mind.
聽輕音樂可以放鬆你的心情。

Unit Thirteen

你值得!

Track 1-3-13

You deserve it!

你值得!

I am so happy for you.

我真為你感到高興。

急用會話

ERIC I got a pay raise!

我加薪了!

EMILY Really?

真的嗎?

ERIC Yes, because I have been working so hard lately.

是啊,因為我最近努力地工作。

EMILY You deserve it!

你值得!

I am so happy for you.

我真為你感到高興。

88

臨 時 用 語

1. 我真是為你感到驕傲：
I am proud of you.
You make me proud.

2. 我相信你很棒：
I believe you are great!

3. 你很有天賦：
You are gifted.
You are talented.

單 字 解 說

1. **deserve** 動詞：應受，該得
例 The outstanding student deserved this honor.
這個傑出的學生應該獲得這份榮譽。

2. **raise** 名詞
例 I am about to ask the boss for a raise.
我要找老闆要求加薪。

Unit FOURTEEN

您先請

英文補給站

Track 1-3-14

After you.
您先請。
Ladies first.
女士優先。
Please queue here.
請在這排隊。

出外搭車，看展覽或是看電影買票，常常我們會遇到需要排隊的時候，這個時候當我們看到 queue here (請在這裡排隊)的招牌時，就知道要從哪開始排隊起。還有，為了避免失禮，在排隊或是過路時，我們也可以說 after you (您先請)。

急用會話

JANE Hey, don't cut! I am in line.
嘿，別插隊！我在排隊。
Please queue here.
在這裡排隊。
JACK Sorry. I did not see the sign.
抱歉，我沒看到標示。

90

臨 時 用 語

1. 在這排隊:
Line up here.

Please line up.

This way, please.

2. 我會在櫃台排隊等你:
I will wait for you in line by the front desk.

3. 不要插隊:
Don't cut in line.

4. 下一個，請:
Next, please.

Go on.

5. 我是要排隊還是要抽號碼牌?:
Do I need to get in the line or take a number?

6. 是在這裡排隊嗎?:
Is this the line?

Unit FIFTEEN
祝福你

 Track 1-3-15

Bless you.
祝福你。

Good luck.
祝好運。

Wish you well.
祝你一切安好。

禮多人不怪，這一個道理也適用於英美的生活
文化。所以祝福的話，如Good luck(祝好運)或
是Bless you(祝福你)，可以用在祝福對方的努
力開花結果，或是一般見面道別，祝福對方安
好，也可以用於信末題詞。

急用會話

FRANK I heard that you got promoted.
我聽說你升職了。

FIONA Yes, and now I am working for a
new project.
是啊，現在我正在著手一個新的企劃。

FRANK Good luck to you.
祝你好運啊。

臨 時 用 語

1. 祝你健康：

Good health.

To health. (多用於敬酒)

2. 新年快樂：

Happy New Year.

3. 聖誕快樂：

Merry Christmas.

I wish you a merry Christmas.

4. 生日快樂：

Happy birthday.

5. 旅途愉快，一路順風：

Bon voyage.

Have a nice trip.

6. 祝你一切順利：

(用於分離，如離職或畢業)

All the best.

Unit SIXTEEN

我真是受寵若驚

英文補給站

I am too flattered.
我真是受寵若驚。
I am happy to hear that.
我真高興聽到你這樣說。

當別人讚美你You are so beautiful. (你真漂亮)，
How nice of you to come! (真高興你來)或是I
cannot imagine my life without you.(沒有你我真
不知道怎麼活下去)之類的話，除了謝謝對方，
我們還可以跟對方說I am too flattered (我真是
受寵若驚)。

急用會話

HEATHER Henry, I cannot believe it.
亨利，我真不敢相信。
You have cleaned the whole office.
你掃完了整間辦公室。
You did a great job!
你做的很棒！
HENRY I am too flattered!
我真是受寵若驚。

臨 時 用 語

1. 這真是令人難以置信:
It's amazing.
It's incredible!

2. 我真是受寵若驚:
You are flattering me.

3. 你太過獎了:
You are just being polite.
You are very kind to say so.

單 字 解 說

1. **flatter** 動詞:諂媚,奉承,調情
   例 Mike likes to flatter his boss.
   麥克喜歡奉承他的老闆。

2. **polite** 形容詞:有禮貌的
   例 It is polite to say "hi" when you meet someone.
   當你遇到人的時候,說聲嗨是有禮貌的。

NOTE BOOK

哈啦最急用 Joining in the Conversation

第四章

臨時急用

請求與協助
Chapter Four Asking For Help

Unit ONE

不好意思，可以請你幫我忙嗎?

 Track 1-4-01

Excuse me, could you help me?

不好意思，可以請你幫我忙嗎?

Would you please do me a favor?

可以請你幫我忙嗎?

俗話說:在家靠父母，出外靠朋友。在外時，當遇到狀況，一句Could you help me? (可以請你幫我忙嗎?)，就是最好用的求救訊息。

急用會話

JASON Excuse me, could you help me, Emily?

不好意思，艾蜜莉，可以請你幫我忙嗎?

EMILY What's the problem?

怎麼了?

JASON My computer just crashed.

我電腦壞了。

EMILY I'll check it.

我會檢查它。

臨 時 用 語

1. 可以請你幫我忙嗎?:

Would you please give me a hand?

Would you do it for me?

Could I ask you a favor?

2. 拜託!:

Come on!

Please!

單 字 解 說

1. help 動詞:幫忙

例 When I am in trouble, my brother always comes to help me.

每當我遭逢困難的時候,我哥總是會來幫我。

2. problem 名詞:問題

例 The students have problems with those math questions.

這些學生算這些數學題有問題。

would跟could有兩種意思,一種是單純的過去式,一種是禮貌性的用字,但用在問句的開頭時,是一種禮貌性的問話,並無過去式的意思。在這些問句中加上excuse me(不好意思)或please(請)會更有禮貌。

請你說慢一點。

英文補給站

 Track 1-4-02

Please speak slowly.
請你說慢一點。
Slowly, please.
請你說慢一點。
What did you say?
你剛說什麼?

因為語言的不同,常常我們跟外國人士溝通交談時,會因為很多因素,一時之間抓不到對方的意思,這時候,不用緊張,只要大聲說出 Slowly, please. (請你說慢一點) ,再請對方慢慢地說一遍就好了。

急用會話

PETER Do you know how to get to the train station?
你知道如何到火車站嗎?

LEE Well, please speak slowly.
呃,請你說慢一點。

PETER How do I get to the train station?
如何到火車站嗎?

LEE Go straight and you will see it.
直走你就會看到了。

臨 時 用 語

1. 再說一遍:

Excuse me!

Pardon?

Please say that again.

Repeat your question again, please.

2. 慢一點:

Slow down, please.

Slowly.

單 字 解 說

1. speak 動詞：說話；講(語言)

例 Helen can speak three languages: Chinese, English, and Thai.

海倫會說三種語言:中文、英文、跟泰文。

2. slowly 副詞

例 He walked slowly because of his bad leg.

他因為腳傷所以行走緩慢。

Unit THREE
請問你會說英文嗎?

 Track 1-4-03

Can you speak English?

請問你會說英文嗎?

English, please.

講英文,好嗎?

英文除了是英美澳加的人士的母語之外,也是國際語言(international language)。所以,去到歐洲或是中南美洲等非英語系國家,或者是在台灣遇到外籍人士,也可以嘗試用英文與他們做基本的日常生活溝通。

急用會話

GINA Excuse me, can you speak English?

不好意思,你會說英文嗎?

JENNY Yes, but my English is poor.

會啊,可是我英文不好。

GINA Come on. That's OK.

拜託,沒關係。

JENNY It's true, so please speak slowly.

這是真的,所以請你講慢一點。

臨 時 用 語

1. 你會說中文嗎?:
Can you speak Chinese?
Please say that in Chinese, please!

2. 我的中文不好:
My Chinese is poor.
My Chinese is bad.

3. 我會說一點中文:
My Chinese is so-so.
I can speak a little bit of Chinese.

4. 我中文說得很好:
My Chinese is fluent.
I can speak Chinese well.

單 字 解 說

世界常用語言英文:

中文: Chinese

日文: Japanese

韓文: Korean

法文: French

西班牙文: Spanish

德文: German

Unit Four
我能跟你談一談嗎?

Can I talk to you?
我能跟你談一談嗎?
Can you spare a minute?
你有空嗎?

當我們渴望跟對方好好聊一聊最近的事,或者是請求對方與我們詳談事情時,我們可以問對方一句Can I talk to you? (我能跟你談一談嗎?)。

STAFF Can you spare a minute this afternoon?
你今天下午可以空出一些時間嗎?
Mr. Wang will be expecting you at 3:00 in his office.
王先生下午三點會在辦公室等你。
DAVID Let me check my schedule.
我查一下我的行程。
OK, three o'clock will be fine with me.
好啊,三點我可以。

臨 時 用 語

1. 你有空嗎?:

Are you free for the moment?

Do you have time?

Are you available now?

2. 我有話要跟你說:

I want to talk to you.

I want say something to you.

單 字 解 說

1. talk 動詞：說話

例 Our boss wants to talk to you about the project.

我們老闆想跟你說一些關於這個案子的事。

2. spare 動詞：空出騰出

例 My mother spared a room for the guest.

我媽空出一間房間給客人。

Ⓤⓝⓘⓣ FIVE
救命!

 Track 1-4-05

Help!
救命!
Somebody help!
請救命!
S.O.S.
救命!

當遇到緊急時刻(emergency)時,直接喊出Help!
是最直接的呼救方式;而SOS(save our soul)更
是許多國家通用的求救信號。

急用會話

FAITH Help!
救命!
Somebody help!
來人救命啊!
This is an emergency!
這是一件緊急的事啊!

臨 時 用 語

1. 救命！：

Please help me.

Give me a hand, please.

Help! I need your help.

單 字 解 說

1. **somebody 代名詞：某人**

   例 Somebody just phoned me.

   剛有人打電話給我。

2. **save 動詞：拯救**

   例 The doctor saves many patients' lives.

   這位醫生救了很多病人的性命。

3. **soul 名詞：靈魂**

   例 When people die, their souls will leave their bodies.

   當人們死去，他們的靈魂會離開他們的身體。

4. **emergency 名詞：緊急的事**

   例 In an emergency, you can dial 911.

   緊急時刻你可以撥打911。

你需要幫忙嗎?

英文補給站 Track 1-4-06

May I help you?

你需要幫忙嗎?

Do you need any help?

你需要幫忙嗎?

If you need my help, just let me know.

如果你需要幫忙嗎,請讓我知道。

很多時候,當我們要對人們表示善意,或伸出援手,就只要問說May I help you? (你需要幫忙嗎?)就可以了。此外May I help you?這句話也是餐廳服務生,博物館服務員常常掛在嘴邊的一句話,所以當聽到時,別忘了適時給予回應喔。

急用會話

JANE You look terrible.

你看起來很糟。

Do you need any help?

你需要幫忙嗎?

MAY I hurt my fingers. I think I need to find the first-aid kit now.

我弄傷了我的手指頭。我想我現在需要找到急救箱。

JANE OK, I will do that for you.

好的，我會幫你。

MAY Thank you.

謝謝。

臨 時 用 語

1. 我能為你做什麼?:

What can I do for you?

What do you need me for?

2. 我想我能幫你:

I think I can help you.

單 字 解 說

1. need 動詞:需要

例 The patient needs to see a doctor.

這一個病人需要去看醫生。

2. hurt 動詞:弄傷

(hurt屬於不規則動詞變化:hurt-hurt-hurt)

例 Jean accidentally hurt herself when she was sewing her jacket.

珍在縫她的夾克時，不小心弄傷她自己。

Unit SEVEN
有沒有問題？

 Track 1-4-07

Any problem?
有沒有問題?
What's the matter?
怎麼回事?
What happened?
發生什麼事了?

這個單元跟Unit Six介紹的句子皆可用於對需要協助的人表示善意，或伸出援手。

急用會話

KIM Jack, you look strange. Are you all right?
傑克，你看起來怪怪的。你還好嗎？

JACK No, I got a hangover.
不好，我宿醉。

KIM What's the matter?
怎麼回事？

JACK I failed the project and felt very bad.
我搞砸了案子而且感覺很糟。

110

臨 時 用 語

1. 發生什麼事了?:

What's going on here?

What's the matter with you?

2. 怎麼回事?:

Anything wrong?

單 字 解 說

1. matter 名詞：問題，事情

例 It is just a matter of time.

這只是遲早的問題。

2. happen 動詞：發生

例 Did you hear what happened? John was

in a car accident this morning.

約翰今天早上發生車禍。

3. strange 形容詞：奇怪的

例 The strange clothes makes Coco look

funny.

可可穿這套奇怪的衣服看起來很可笑。

Unit Eight

要我幫你帶點東西嗎?

英文補給站

 Track 1-4-08

Do you need me to bring you something?
要我幫你帶點東西嗎?

You can count on me.
你可以依賴我。

當你要出門辦點事或買東西,可順口問一下
同事或朋友家人Do you need me to bring you
something? (要我幫你帶點東西嗎?),順便幫忙
他們帶點東西回來。

急用會話

ARIEL Mom, I am going to do some
shopping.
媽,我要去買點東西。

Do you need me to bring you something?
要我幫你帶點東西回來嗎?

JOYCE I need some vegetables and soy
sauce to make dinner.
我需要一些菜跟醬油做晚餐。

Could you bring me some?
你能幫我帶點回來嗎?

ARIEL Sure, you can count on me.
可以啊,你可以依賴我。

112

臨 時 用 語

1. 你要什麼?:

What do you want?

What would you like?

Do you need anything?

Can I get you anything?

2. 我來處理就好:

Allow me.

單 字 解 說

1. bring 動詞：帶來

(bring為不規則動詞變化:bring-brought-brought)

例 The typhoon brought heavy rain.

這個颱風帶來的暴雨。

2. count on 動詞：片語依賴；信賴

例 Fred counts on his bother because he is very reliable.

弗來德信賴她哥哥因為他很可靠。

你要一起來嗎?

英文補給站

 Track 1-4-09

Do you want to come along?

你要一起來嗎?

Come on.

一起來嘛!

Let's go.

一起來嘛!

當你要出門參加活動或遊玩時,可以順口問一下同事或朋友家人Do you want to come along? (你要一起來嗎?),邀約他們同行。

急用會話

ROY Joe, are you free this afternoon?

喬,你今天下午有空嗎?

JOE Yeah, but why do you ask?

有啊,你幹嘛問?

ROY My colleagues and I are going to watch a basketball game.

我同事跟我要去看棒球賽。

Do you want to come along?

你要一起來嗎?

JOE OK.

好啊。

臨 時 用 語

1. 要跟嗎:

Come with us!

Join us!

In or out?

Do you want to join us?

How about coming with us?

單 字 解 說

1. watch 動詞:帶來

例 Many people like to watch TV after work.

很多人下班喜歡看電視。

2. basketball 名詞:籃球

例 Many Taiwanese like to watch basketball games.

很多台灣人喜歡看棒球賽。

3. join 動詞:參加

例 Kelvin joined that summer camp last year.

凱文去年參加了那個夏令營。

𝖀nit TEN
抱歉，恐怕不行

英文補給站

 Track 1-4-10

Sorry. I'm afraid I can't.
抱歉，恐怕不行。
No, I am sorry.
不行，抱歉。
I'm too tired.
我很累。

當他人請求協助，而自己卻也分身乏術，或沒有意願幫忙時，我們可以直接說No,I am sorry.(不行，抱歉)。或者是委婉地說Sorry. I'm afraid I can't. (抱歉，恐怕不行)，來表示拒絕。

急用會話

ARIEL Do you go back home?
你要回家嗎？
Could you give me a ride?
你可以讓我搭個便車嗎？
BILLY Sorry. I'm afraid I can't.
抱歉，恐怕不行。
I'm too tired.
我很累。

116

臨 時 用 語

1. 抱歉，我不行:
Sorry, but I don't think that I can.

2. 抱歉，我明天很忙:
Sorry, but I'm busy tomorrow.

3. 恐怕不行:
That will not be possible.

4. 等一下，讓我想想:
Just a moment! Let me think a second.
I'll think about it.

單 字 解 說

1. afraid 形容詞：害怕的
例 The little girl is afraid of the dark.

這個小女孩怕黑。

2. tired 形容詞：疲累的
例 After one day's hard work, Kirby felt very
tired.

一天辛苦工作之後，克比覺得很累。

很抱歉，我處理不來

英文補給站 Track 1-4-11

Sorry, but I cannot handle it.

抱歉，但我處理不來。

I am sorry to turn you down.

抱歉，我要拒絕你。

I am not in the mood.

我沒那個心情。

本單元介紹的句子跟Unit Ten一樣，可用於當我們要拒絕協助他人或是他人的邀約。但本章的語氣較為堅決直接，要注意使用的場合。

急用會話

LEO Can you help me copy 50 pages of this document?

你可以幫我影印五十份這份文件嗎？

LISA I am busy with my work. Can't you see that?

我正忙著處理我的工作，你難道沒看到嗎？

LEO Please!

拜託！

LISA Sorry, but I cannot handle it.

抱歉，但我處理不來。

臨 時 用 語

1. 我拒絕：

I refuse.

No way!

2. 沒什麼好說的：

There is nothing to talk about.

3. 我要是可以我就會幫你：

If I could, I would.

單 字 解 說

1. turn down 動詞：片語拒絕

例 The editor's proposal was turned down.

這一個編輯的提案被拒絕了。

2. mood 名詞：心情

例 Frank is in a good mood because it is sunny.

因為今天天氣晴所以法蘭克心情很好。

3. busy 形容詞

例 I am busy washing the dishes.

我忙著洗碗。

Unit TWELVE
小事一件!

Track 1-4-12

All right.
可以。

Don't mention it!
小事一件!

My pleasure.
我的榮幸。

當他人請求協助,而自己也有意願幫忙時,我們可以欣然地說一句All right. (可以),來回應他人的詢問,表示我們要答應或同意給予他人協助。

急用會話

LYDIA Katy, I lost my purse this morning.
凱蒂,我今天早上掉了錢包。

May I borrow 500 dollars from you?
我可以跟你借五百元嗎?

KATY All right! Here you are.
可以。這裡。

LYDIA Thank you.
謝謝。

臨 時 用 語

1. 別介意:

Never mind.

It's no big deal.

My word!

2. 別擔心:

Don't worry.

單 字 解 說

1. pleasure 名詞

例 I find great pleasure in listening to music.

我從聽音樂中得到很大的樂趣。

2. purse 名詞:(女用)提包

例 The purse is made of real leather.

這個包包是真皮做的。

3. borrow 動詞:(從⋯)借

例 May I borrow a pen from you?

可以跟你借支筆嗎?

Unit THIRTEEN
我可以

It is fine with me.
我可以。
I would like to.
我很樂意。

本單元介紹的句子跟Unit Twelve一樣,可用於表示同意協助他人或是答應他人的邀約。

急用會話

KAREN Amy, are you available this Friday night?
艾咪,你這星期五有空嗎?

ARIEL Why do you ask?
為什麼這麼問?

KAREN I am wondering if you can come to teach me math.
我在想說你可以來教我數學嗎。

ARIEL It is fine with me.
我可以。

I will have dinner with my parents first and then I will go to help you.
我會先跟我父母親用完晚餐,然後再去幫你。

臨 時 用 語

1. 我很樂意：
I would love to.

2. 你說了算：
You are the boss.

3. 那應該可以：
That would be fine.

單 字 解 說

1. available 形容詞：可獲得的；有空的
例 Susan is available only on the weekend.
蘇珊只有周末有空。

2. fine 形容詞：好的；行得通的
例 That offer is fine with me.
這項提案對我而言都可以。

3. boss 名詞：老闆
例 The boss is kind to his employees.
這個老闆對他的員工很好。

Unit Fourteen

太好了

 Track 1-4-14

That will be nice.

太好了。

That will be great.

太棒了。

I really appreciate it.

實在感謝。

當我們請求他人協助，而別人也欣然同意或是熱心地幫了我們一個大忙，我們要說一聲That will be great. (太棒了)來感謝他人同意提供協助與邀約。

急用會話

MARY Those bags are really heavy. My hands hurt badly.

這些袋子真的好重。我的雙手真痛。

MARTIN May I help you carry some of these bags?

我可以幫你提一些袋子嗎?

MARY Really? Thank you. That will be nice.

真的嗎?謝謝。真是太好了。

臨 時 用 語

1. 你實在太好了:

That would be very nice of you.

2. 我欠你一次:

I owe you one.

3. 我要怎麼報答你呢?:

How can I repay you?

單 字 解 說

1. appreciate 動詞:感謝

例 Jack deeply appreciates his father's support.

傑克很感謝他父親的支持。

2. heavy 形容詞:沉重的

例 Mike moved the heavy boxes into the warehouse.

麥克把這些重重的箱子搬進倉庫。

3. carry 動詞:提;扛;搬

例 Don't forget to carry an umbrella with you.

別忘了帶雨傘。

NOTE
BOOK

Ladies and gentlemen, welcome to our hotel, where
Do you need any help?
I need some vegetables and
Many students like to stay at home
How about coming with u

It is a conversation that in big

哈啦最急用 Joining in the Conversation

第五章

臨時
急用

交友
Chapter Five Making Friends

e vegeta
students like to stay at ho
coming with us?
that my birthday is the same as hers

Unit ONE
很高興認識你

Nice to meet you.
很高興認識你。
Nice to meet you, too.
我也很高興認識你。
This is Mark.
這是馬克。

當兩個陌生人初相識的打招呼與介紹，沒有什麼比一句比Nice to meet you.(很高興認識你)更容易破冰，並同時表示禮貌跟榮幸相識。依西方禮儀還會互相握手。

急用會話

TIM Jason, this is Mark, my best friend.
傑生，這是馬克，我最好的朋友。
Mark, this is Jason, my brother.
馬克，這是傑生，我弟弟。
MARK Nice to meet you.
很高興認識你。
JASON Nice to meet you, too.
我也很高興認識你。

128

臨 時 用 語

1. 很高興認識你:

Good to see you.

I am happy to see you.

I am pleased to see you.

2. 家人相關單字

father 父親

mother 母親

brother 兄弟

sister 姊妹

uncle 叔,伯,舅

grandfather 祖父(外公)

grandmother 祖母(外婆)

aunt 姑,姨,嬸

單 字 解 說

1. friend 名詞:朋友

例 Mary is my friend.
瑪莉是我的朋友。

2. too 副詞:也

例 Many people in Taiwan can speak Chinese; they can speak English, too.
很多在台灣的人會說中文,也會說英文。

$\mathcal{U}nit$ Two
我們以前見過嗎?

Have we met before?
我們以前見過嗎?
You are?
你是?
I didn't recognize you!
我都不認出你來了!

如果突然發現對方是自己失散多年的好友的
話,就可以應用本單元介紹的句子。

急用會話

WAYNE Have we met before?
我們以前見過嗎?

WINNIE You are?
你是?

WAYNE I am Wayne, your classmate in
senior high.
我是偉恩,你高中同學。

WINNIE You have totally changed! I can
hardly recognize you!
你變真多,我幾乎都不認出你來了!

130

臨 時 用 語

1. 我們以前見過嗎?:

Have we ever met before?

Haven't I met you before?

2. 我都不認出你來了!:

I cannot recognize you.

I didn't know it was you!

3. 你不記得我喔?:

Don't you remember me?

Don't you recognize me?

4. 你變好多:

You've changed a lot.

單字解說

1. **remember** 動詞：記得;想起

例 Do you remember Emily's email address?

你記得艾蜜莉的電郵地址嗎?

2. **recognize** 動詞：認出;識別

例 The witness recognized the man as the murderer.

證人認出來這個男生是謀殺犯。

Unit THREE
你真的好體貼喔

英文補給站

 Track 1-5-03

You are so considerate.
你真的好體貼喔。
You are so kind.
你人真好。
You are a genius.
你真是天才。

急用會話

SIMON Surprise! Here is your birthday gift.
驚喜!這是你的生日禮物。
SELINA Wow, it is such a beautiful necklace.
哇,真是一條漂亮的項鍊。
SIMON I hope you will like it.
我希望你會喜歡。
SELINA You are so considerate.
你真的好體貼喔。

臨 時 用 語

1. 你真的好體貼喔:
You are so caring.

You are really thoughtful.

2. 你人真好:
You are a good person.

It is so nice of you.

3. 你真是天才:
You are smart.

You are brilliant.

單 字 解 說

1. considerate 形容詞：體貼的
例 Kirby is very considerate to everyone in the company.

克比對公司每個人都很體貼。

2. necklace 名詞：項鍊
例 Jane bought a necklace as her husband's birthday gift.

珍買了一條項鍊當做她先生的生日禮物。

Unit FOUR
他很可愛

英文補給站

Track 1-5-04

He is cute.
他很可愛。
He is handsome.
他很帥。
He is adorable.
他很可愛。

見到要表示好感或有興趣的男生，除了可以用常聽到的He is cool. (他真酷)來稱讚之外，我們可以還可以用本單元介紹的句子稱讚他很可愛。

急用會話

JESSIE Look, it is John.
看哪，那是約翰。
JENNIFER Yes, and he is the most eligible bachelor in the office.
是啊，他可是我們辦公室最有價值的單身漢呢。
JESSIE Yeah, I cannot agree more.
是啊，我同意。
He is so cute.
他很可愛。

臨 時 用 語

1. 他很帥：

He is gorgeous.

He is fine.

He is awesome.

2. 我同意：

I agree.

I can never agree with you too much.

單 字 解 說

1. cute 形容詞：可愛

例 Kathy is a cute little girl.

凱西是一個可愛的女孩。

2. handsome 形容詞：帥

例 The newcomer looks very handsome.

這一個新進員工看起來很帥。

Unit FIVE
她真特別

Track 1-5-05

She is special.
她真特別。
She is sweet.
她真甜。

當見到漂亮的女生，我們除了可以She is cute. (她真可愛)或是She is beautiful .(她真美麗)來稱讚之外，我以還可以用本單元介紹的句子來表示有好感或有興趣。

急用會話

PETER Hey, Andy. Is that your colleague, May?
嘿，安迪。那是你的同事，梅，嗎？

ANDY Yes, she works in the public relationships department.
是啊，她在公關部工作。

PETER She is special.
她真特別。

ANDY Oh, you seem to like her.
喔，你似乎喜歡她。

136

1. 她真特別:

She is unique.

She is one of a kind.

2. 她真漂亮:

She is pretty.

She is beautiful.

She is stunning.

3. 她很性感:

She is sexy.

She is hot.

4. 她真是一個可愛的女生!:

What a cute girl she is!

5. 她笑容真迷人!:

How lovely her smile is!

Unit SIX

我迷上她了

I have a crush on her.
我迷上她了。

We have chemistry.
我們有化學反應。

She makes me feel so special.
她讓我覺得很特別。

當想要用英文表示對某人有特殊的感覺或者是很喜歡，我們就可以說I have a crush on her.(我迷上她了)，直接來表達愛意。要注意的是，我們常常聽到的I fall in love with you.通常指的是雙方之間已經有一定的認識而已陷入熱戀。

急用會話

HENRY Do you remember Judy, the girl we met in the pub last night?
你還記得裘蒂嗎? 就是我們昨晚在小酒館遇到的女生。

FRED Yeah, she is really cute and funny.
記得啊，她很可愛而且風趣。

HENRY Yeah, I think I have a crush on her.
是啊，我想我迷上她了。

138

臨 時 用 語

1. 我迷上她了:

I have a big crush on her.

I'm all over her.

2. 我沒有你沒辦法活下去:

I can't live without you.

3. 你使我完整:

You make me whole. You complete me.

4. 我愛你:

I love you.

單 字 解 說

1. crush 名詞:迷戀

例 Beatrice has a secret crush on her colleague.

碧翠絲偷偷的迷上她同事。

2. chemistry 名詞:化學(衍生為「來電」)

例 My favorite subject is chemistry.

我最喜歡的科目是化學。

Unit SEVEN

她喜歡什麼?

Track 1-5-07

What does she like?
她喜歡什麼?
What is his hobby?
他有什麼嗜好?

當對對方有好感,想要進一步詢問對方的興趣以及嗜好,就可以向她的朋友問一句What does she like? (她喜歡什麼?)。

急用會話

LEO Judy, is Mandy in your department?
裘蒂,曼蒂在你的部門嗎?

JUDY Yes, but why do you ask?
是啊,但你幹嘛問啊?

LEO Well. I just think she is special.
沒事,我只是覺得她很特別。

JUDY Oh, you like her!
喔,你喜歡上她了!

LEO Sort of. What does she like?
算是吧。她喜歡什麼?

JUDY I suppose she likes dancing much.
我想她很喜歡跳舞。

1. **他是一個足球迷:**

He is a football fan.

He is a fan of football.

2. **我覺得溜冰很有趣:**

I think skating is interesting.

3. **常見運動英文:**

自行車: cycling　衝浪: surfing

籃球: basketball　棒球: baseball

游泳: swimming　瑜珈: yoga

有氧舞蹈: Aerobics　撞球: pool

板球: cricket　慢跑: jogging

排球: volleyball　保齡球: bowling

網球: tennis　浮潛: snorkeling

皮拉堤斯: Pilates　羽球: badminton

水肺潛水: scuba diving

極限運動: extreme sport

輪鞋溜冰: roller-skating

滑板運動: skateboarding

Unit EIGHT

今晚一起去喝一杯吧?

英文補給站

 Track 1-5-08

How about a drink tonight?
今晚一起去喝一杯吧?
How about having dinner together tonight?
今晚一起用餐吧?
Are you free this Saturday?
你這個星期六有空嗎?

當對對方有好感,想要進一步邀約對方,我們可以問How about a drink tonight? (今晚一起去喝一杯吧?)或是Are you free this Saturday? (你這個星期六有空嗎?)。

急用會話

OLIVER Olivia, how about a drink tonight?
奧利維亞,今晚一起去喝一杯吧?
OLIVIA OK, I am free tonight. Where do you want to meet?
好啊,我今晚有空。你要約那裡見面?
OLIVER How about Sandy's?
在仙蒂絲餐廳好嗎?
OLIVIA OK, I will see you at six.

好啊，我們六點見囉。

臨 時 用 語

1. 我們今晚一起去看電影吧?：

Why don't we watch a film tonight?

How about watching a film tonight?

2. 我們今晚一起去看電影喝咖啡吧?：

Why don't we have coffee tonight?

How about having coffee tonight?

3. 你明天有空嗎?：

Are you free tomorrow?

Are you available tomorrow?

4. 我們今晚要做什麼呢?：

What shall we do tonight?

5. 你來接我好嗎?：

Will you pick me up?

6. 我會在那兒：

I will be right there.

Unit NINE
我們只是朋友

Track 1-5-09

We are just friends.
我們只是朋友。
I am not attracted to you.
你不吸引我。

當他人對你示好，而你一點意思都沒有，又不想直接說一句 I don't like you.(我不喜歡你) 來表示自己的態度與立場；那麼，We are just friends. (我們只是朋友)會是一句很好發好人卡的一句英文。

急用會話

JACK I like you, Rose.
我喜歡你，羅絲。
ROSS Thank you.
謝謝。
I'm not attracted to you.
你不吸引我。
I think we still can be friends.
我們還可以是朋友。

144

臨 時 用 語

1. 我真的配不上你：

I don't deserve you.

2. 我們兩個不配：

We don't match each other.

3. 你值得更好的：

You deserve someone better.

4. 他被拒絕了：

He got turned down.

He was rejected.

5. 天涯何處無芳草：

There are plenty of fish in the sea.

單 字 解 說

1. attract 動詞：吸引

例 The smell of candy attracts lots of ants.

糖果的香味吸引了很多螞蟻。

你不是我的菜

英文補給站 Track 1-5-10

You are not my type.
你不是我的喜歡的型。
He is not my cup of tea.
他不是我的菜。

現在年輕人常常會向他們沒有興趣而卻對他們
表示好感的人說:你不是我的菜!而在英文中,
因為英國悠久飲茶習慣的影響,我們會說You
are not my cup of tea (你不是我的茶)來對示好
的人表示沒有進一步的興趣。

急用會話

LYDIA Did you meet Jim, the transfer
student, in the school this morning?
你今天早上有在學校遇到轉學生吉姆嗎?

LINDA Yeah. He looks tall, cute, and
cool.
有啊,他看起來又高又可愛又酷。
I think he is charming.
我覺得他好迷人。

LYDIA But he is not friendly. He is not
my type.
但是他不友善耶。他不是我的菜。

臨 時 用 語

1. 你不是我的真命天子：

You are not my Prince of Charming.

You are not my Mr. Right.

2. 你不是我的真命天女：

You are not my Ms. Right.

單 字 解 說

1. type 名詞：類型，樣式

例 What type of book do you like to read?

你喜歡讀什麼種類的書?

2. tea 名詞：茶

例 Do you like fruit tea?

你喜歡水果茶嗎?

3. charming 形容詞：迷人的

例 Your smile is really charming.

你的笑容真迷人。

你太八卦了啦!

英文補給站

Track 1-5-11

You are so gossipy.
你太八卦了啦!

I cannot stand it anymore.
我沒辦法再忍下去了!

八卦(閒話)在英文就叫做gossip,而愛說八卦的樣子就叫做gossipy。當我們要想他人表示他真的是太長舌了,就可以用本單元介紹的句子。

急用會話

JEAN Anna, you know what?
安娜,你知道嗎?

Colby just has an affair with his colleague.
科比跟他同事有外遇。

I am gonna tell Maria the sad news.
我要去跟瑪麗亞說這一件壞消息。

ANNA Stop! I cannot stand it anymore.
我沒辦法再忍下去了!

You are so gossipy.
你太八卦了啦!

臨 時 用 語

1. 你真是愛說話:

You are chatty.

You are really talkative.

2. 我忍不下去了啦:

I cannot bear it anymore.

I cannot put up with you any longer.

I can no longer stand it.

單 字 解 說

1. gossip 名詞：八卦;閒話

例 Stacy shaned the gossip with her
classmates.

史黛西跟她同學閒話了一下。

2. stand 動詞：忍受

例 I cannot stand the heat in summer.

我沒辦法忍受夏天的熱。

Unit TWELVE
我們昨天吵架了

We had a fight yesterday.

我們昨天吵架了。

We had a quarrel.

我們吵架了。

We decided to break up.

我們決定分手。

如果交往之後發現個性不合，面臨吵架，分手，就可以用一句 We decided to break up. (我們決定分手) 來解釋你交往的狀態。

急用會話

MAGGIE Cindy, how are you? You look awful!

辛蒂，你還好嗎?你看起來糟透了!

Did you sleep well last night?

你昨晚有睡好嗎?

CINDY No. I am very sad because Tom and I had a fight yesterday.

沒有。我好傷心，因為我跟湯姆昨晚吵了一架。

MAGGIE Poor you.

你真可憐。

臨 時 用 語

1. 他拋棄我了：

He dumped me.

2. 我跟我男朋友分手了：

I broke up with my boyfriend.

3. 我們分手了：

We broke up.

We ended our relationship.

單 字 解 說

1. fight 名詞：吵架；打架

例 These two brothers had a fight for a robot.

這兩兄弟為了一隻機器人打架。

2. quarrel 名詞：吵架

例 Jack had a quarrel with his classmate.

傑克跟他同學吵架了。

3. break up 動詞：片語分手

例 Kelly broke up with her partner last night.

凱利昨晚跟她的夥伴分手了。

你是不是正在和別人交往？

英文補給站

 Track 1-5-13

Are you seeing someone?
你是不是正在和別人交往？
Are you dating John?
你正和約翰交往嗎？
I am dating someone.
我現正交往中。

當暗戀某人已久，頻頻示愛，卻又沒有收到明
確回應，不知如何開口時，就可以直接問Are
you seeing someone? See在這裡不只是「看」
的意思，更有「交往」之意。

急用會話

TOM Sue, you are looking glamorous recently.
蘇，你最近看起來美極了。
Are you seeing someone?
你是有和誰交往嗎？
SUE Hey, it's none of your business.
嘿，這跟你沒關係！

臨 時 用 語

1. 我現正交往中:

I'm in a relationship.

I'm seeing someone.

2. 我有男朋友了:

I have a boyfriend.

3. 我有女朋友了:

I have a girlfriend.

單 字 解 說

1. date 動詞:交往

例 Romeo is dating his classmate.

羅密歐正和他同學交往。

2. relationship 名詞:關係

例 It is not easy to manage a relationship.

經營一段關係不容易。

3. boyfriend 名詞:男朋友

例 Jean has a boyfriend.

珍有一個男友。

NOTE
BOOK

哈啦最急用 Joining in the Conversation

第六章

臨時急用

狀況不佳時
Chapter Six Feeling Poor

Unit ONE
我不知道耶

Track 1-6-01

I have no idea.
我不知道耶。
I don't know.
我不知道。
I am not sure.
我不確定。

當有人詢問你事情,或是問你的意見,而你忘了或者是不想回答時,就可以說一句Sorry, but I have no idea. (抱歉,但我不知道耶)。

急用會話

FIONA You know what?
你知道嗎?
KIM What?
什麼?
FIONA Diana and her husband divorced two days ago.
黛安娜跟她先生兩天前離婚了
KIM I don't know that, but I am sorry to hear that.
我不知道耶,但是我很遺憾聽到這個消息。

156

臨 時 用 語

1. 我不知道：
I have no clue.

I don't have the slightest idea.

2. 我很遺憾：
I feel sorry about it.

Sorry.

單 字 解 說

1. idea 名詞：想法
例 There are a lot of interesting ideas in this book.

這本書裡有很多有趣的想法。

2. know 動詞：知道
(know為不規則動詞變化:know—knew—known)

例 Mandy knew the bad news.

曼蒂已經知道這一個壞消息。

3. sorry 形容詞：遺憾的
例 Margret felt sorry for her sister because she just got fired.

瑪格莉特為他妹妹被解雇感到遺憾。

𝔘nit Two
我不是故意的

Track 1-6-02

I didn't not mean it.
我不是故意的。
Pardon me.
原諒我。
Forgive me!
原諒我!

當不小心做錯事情,要祈求他人的原諒時,
我們就可以誠懇真心地說一句I do not mean it.
Forgive me! (我不是故意的, 原諒我!)。

急用會話

RICA Ouch! You tramped on my foot!
啊!你踩到我的腳了!
RICHARD I am sorry. I didn't mean it.
我很抱歉,我不是故意的。
Forgive me!
原諒我!
RICA Forget it.
算了。

臨 時 用 語

1. 我不是故意要傷你：
I do not mean to hurt you.

2. 我不是故意要這樣做：
I do not intend to do so.

I did not do that on purpose.

3. 這是意外：
It's an accident.

單 字 解 說

1. mean 動詞：意指，意圖
(mean為不規則動詞變化:mean—meant—meant)

例 The present is meant for Claudia.
這個禮物是要給克勞蒂雅的。

2. forgive 動詞：原諒
(forgive為不規則動詞變化:forgive—forgave—forgiven)

例 Lance forgave his brother for he sincerely apologized to him.
蘭斯原諒他弟，因為他很真心的跟他道歉了。

Unit THREE
我好沮喪

英文補給站

Track 1-6-03

I am upset.
我好心煩。
I am frustrated.
我好沮喪。
I feel blue.
我很憂鬱。

每個人或多或少都會有心情低落的時候，這時候淡淡地一句I feel blue.(我很憂鬱)，就可以清楚向他人表達我們心情狀態不佳。

急用會話

EMILY You look bad. How are you?
你看起來很糟，你還好嗎？

ELLIS I feel frustrated because I just got fired.
我感覺好沮喪，因為我剛被炒魷魚。

EMILY Sorry to hear that but are you OK?
遺憾聽到這件事，但是你還好嗎？

ELLIS No, I think I need some personal space.
不好，我想我現在需要一些個人空間。

臨 時 用 語

1. 我心情不好：

I am sad.

I am in a bad mood.

I am in low spirits.

I am depressed.

I am under the weather.

2. 我爛透了：

I feel like a loser.

單 字 解 說

1. upset 形容詞：苦惱的；心煩的

   例 Judy was upset over her father's illness.

   裘蒂為了她爸爸的疾病而心煩。

2. frustrated 形容詞：沮喪的；挫敗的

   例 The school team was frustrated after they lost three games in a row.

   連輸了三場比賽之後，整個校隊覺得很挫敗。

英文補給站

 Track 1-6-04

I am tired.
我累了。
She looked totally exhausted.
她看起來一整個精疲力盡。
Be careful not to fall ill.
小心別生病了。

人是肉做的，工作多了，操勞久了，身體難免
會累了，倦了。而一句I am tired.(我累了)，就
可以向對方表達自己身體累壞了。

急用會話

IVAN How are you? You look really
tired.
你還好嗎？你看起來很累。
CHARLOTTE My boss asked me to finish
a big project today.
我老闆今天叫我完成一個大案子。
It took me 12 hours!
那花了我12個小時！
IVAN Wow, it's quite a tough job.
哇，那真是一個艱困的工作。

臨 時 用 語

1. 我累了：

I am fatigued.

I am worn-out.

I am weary.

2. 你看起來沒什麼氣色：

You look pale.

3. 休息吧：

Take a rest.

Take a break.

Rest.

All you need is rest.

Take a day off. (請假一天吧)

4. 保重：

Take care.

Unit FIVE
我不舒服

I feel ill.

我不舒服。

I don't feel well.

我不舒服。

I feel terrible.

我感覺很糟。

人總會有身體欠安、不舒服的時候，這時候一句 I feel ill.(我不舒服)，就可以讓別人知道你身體正在不舒服或是生病了。

急用會話

ERIC John, how are you? You look awful.

約翰，你還好嗎?你看起來很糟。

JOHN I feel ill and my throat hurts.

我不舒服，而且我喉嚨痛。

I think I caught a cold.

我想我感冒了。

ERIC Then, you should take a day off.

那麼，你應該請假一天了。

臨 時 用 語

1. 我(感覺)＿＿＿: I feel ＿＿＿.
   糟糕的: awful   癢: itchy
   痛: painful   受傷: hurt
   痠痛: sore   昏昏的: dizzy
   不舒服: uncomfortable

2. 我有＿＿＿: I have a ＿＿＿.
   頭痛: headache   胃痛: stomachache
   感冒: flu   發燒: fever
   喉嚨痛: sore throat   咳嗽: cough
   著涼: cold   中暑: heat stroke
   受傷: injury   流鼻涕: runny nose
   擦傷: scrape   扭傷: twist
   割傷: cut   傷口: wound

3. 我＿＿＿: I ＿＿＿.
   癢: itch   痛: hurt   嘔吐: vomit
   流血: bleed   流鼻涕: sneeze
   咳嗽: cough   疼痛: ache

Unit SIX
我很擔心

 Track 1-6-06

I am worried.
我很擔心。
What should I do?
我該怎麼辦?

在壓力之下,人除了身體的疲累,心情也會受到影響,會擔心焦慮事情的發展。一句 I am worried. (我很擔心)就可以即時表達我們的心情。

急用會話

WAYNE Shoot! I don't have my wallet with me!
天哪,我的錢包不在身上。
I may have lost it somewhere!
我可能是把它落在哪兒了!

CARLOS Are you kidding!
你在開玩笑嗎?

Wayne: No, it is true and I am worried.
是真得,而且我很擔心。

CARLOS Let's call 911 now.
我們先打911吧。

(＊美國警局電話號碼跟台灣119不同,他們的

166

是911。)

臨 時 用 語

1. 我很擔心:
I am concerned.

2. 我好焦慮:
I am anxious.

3. 振作:
Cheer up.
Chin up.

4. 想想辦法啊！:
Do something.

5. 慢慢來！:
Take your time.

6. 事情會好轉的:
Things will get better.

Unit SEVEN
我忍不下去了

I cannot stand it!
我忍不下去了。
I cannot put up with it!
我忍不下去了。
Stop!
停!

當別人做一些讓我們忍受不了的事情,我們可以告訴他們 I cannot stand it! (我忍不下去了) 來告知別人我們的情緒,並要求他們停止正在做的事。

急用會話

JOE I cannot stand it!
我忍不下去了。
Wade, would you please turn down your MP3 player?
韋德,請你把你的MP3關小聲一點好嗎?
It is really annoying.
那真的很煩人。

WADE I didn't know it is so loud to you.
I will turn it off now.
我不知道這對你是那麼大聲,我現在會把

它關掉。

臨 時 用 語

1. 我忍不下去了:

I cannot bear it.

I cannot tolerate it.

I cannot endure it anymore.

I've run out of patience.

2. 停下來好嗎?:

Would you please stop?

Stop, please.

單 字 解 說

1. turn down 動詞:關小(音量)

例 Please turn down the radio because the baby is sleeping.

請把收音機關小聲一點,因為寶寶正在睡覺。

2. turn off 動詞:關掉(開關)

例 Please turn off the light when you leave.

當你離開時,請記得關燈。

3. tolerate 動詞:容忍

例 Many people cannot tolerate the heat in summer.

很多人無法忍受夏天的炎熱。

Unit EIGHT
冷靜下來!

Calm down!
冷靜下來!
Take it easy.
放鬆點吧!
Just relax.
放鬆吧。

當我們面對沮喪壓力憤怒,無論是他人或是自己,都可以說一句Calm down.(冷靜下來),讓自己淡定。

急用會話

CALVIN You won't believe this.
你不會相信這件事的。
Jack got promoted because he stole
Jess's idea.
傑克升職是因為他偷了潔絲的點子。
SEAN Really? He is such a cheater! I
am gonna tell Jess this.
真的嗎?他真是個欺騙者。我要跟潔絲講這件事。
CALVIN Calm down.
冷靜下來。

臨 時 用 語

1. 算了啦!：
Forget it.
Let it be.

2. 冷靜下來：
Compose yourself.
Don't lose your mind.

3. 放鬆點吧：
Don't take it too hard.

單 字 解 說

1. relax 動詞：使…放鬆
例 Listening to soft music can help us relax.
聽輕音樂可以幫助我們放鬆身心。

2. calm 動詞：使…鎮定
例 The medicine can help calm our nerve system.
這種藥可以幫忙鎮定我們的神經系統。

你也控制一下

 Track 1-6-09

Control yourself.

你也控制一下。

What's wrong with you?

你有毛病啊?

You are helpless!

你真是無藥可救!

當對方的行為越來越脫序,一句禮貌性的Stop, please.也制止不住時,直接跟對方說Control yourself. (你也控制一下),讓對方知道我們心中的不悅跟他行為已經超乎控制。

急用會話

ADAM Andy, look! This TV show is really funny.

安迪,你看那個電視節目真的很有趣。

ANDY What's wrong with you? You are laughing too loud.

你有毛病啊? 你笑的真的很大聲。

Control yourself.

你也控制一下。

ADAM Sorry, but I cannot help it.

抱歉,但我就是忍不住。

臨 時 用 語

1. 你瘋了嗎？：

Are you crazy?

Are you out of your mind?

Are you insane?

2. 控制一下情緒：

Don't lose your head.

Keep your temper under control.

3. 別那樣！：

Don't be that way!

4. 我就是忍不住：

I cannot help it.

I have no choice.

5. 別逼我！：

Don't push me !

6. 閉嘴：

Shut up.

Unit TEN

我受不了了！

I can't take it anymore.

我受不了了！

Get the hell out of here!

滾開！

Enough is enough!

夠了夠了！

本章介紹的句子跟 Unit 9 功能類似，都是用於表達自己對對方失序的行為的不耐，要注意的是，本章的句子非常不禮貌，使用時須注意場合跟與對方的關係。

急用會話

SUSAN Sam, stop singing so loudly!

山姆，停止大聲唱歌！

I am preparing for my final exam.

我正在準備期末考。

SAM Get off my back, and cut it out.

少跟我囉嗦，省省吧！

You can always find another place to study!

你可以找其他的地方讀書啊！

SUSAN I can't take it anymore!

174

我受不了了！

1. 饒了我吧：

Give me a break.

2. 我快氣死啦：

I am angry.

I'm about to explode!

I'm not going to put up with this!

3. 你去死吧！：

Go to hell.

Drop dead.

4. 別煩我：

Don't bother me.

Leave me alone.

Get away from me!

5. 別那樣和我說話！：

Don't talk to me like that!

Don't give me your attitude.

Knock it off.

Unit ELEVEN
別把我惹毛了!

Don't get on my nerves!

別把我惹毛了!

Be quiet!

安靜點!

有時候當他人的行為已經嚴重影響到我們的作息或是心情時,我們可以說Don't get on my nervs!(別把我惹毛了!),來告知對方我們不悅的心情並警告。

急用會話

JACK Tony, what's wrong with you?

湯尼,你有毛病嗎?

Why do you turn up the music?

你幹嘛音樂開那麼大聲?

It is really noisy!

真的很吵耶!

TONY Don't you think this song is really great!

你不覺得這首歌真的很棒嗎?

JACK Turn it down! You're getting on my nerve!

把音樂關小聲!別把我惹毛了!

176

臨 時 用 語

1. 我說的還不夠清楚嗎?:

Is that clear?

Do I make myself clear?

Do you hear me?

2. 規矩一點:

Behave.

Act your age.

3. 你氣死我了啦:

You make me so mad.

You piss me off. (非常不正式的用法)

4. 你真丟人!:

You're a disgrace.

You're an asshole. (非常不正式的用法)

5. 你真不應該那樣做!:

You shouldn't have done that!

Unit TWELVE

別太過分好嗎?

Don't push me around, OK?

別太過分好嗎?

It's not my shit.

干我屁事(非常不正式)。

This is too much for me.

太過分了。

當遇到真的很過分的事情,我們可以用本章的句子來表達不滿。要注意的是這些句子十分口語化,一定不要在正式場合使用,因為十分不客氣。

急用會話

LILY Mandy, can you help my copy these documents?

曼蒂,你可以幫我影印這些文件嗎?

MANDY You have already asked me to do a lot of things for you today.

你今天已經叫我幫你做多事情了。

Don't push me around, OK?

別太過分好嗎?

LILY Sorry.

抱歉。

臨 時 用 語

1. 誰在乎啊:
Who cares!

I don't give the shit.

Who says?

2. 不干我的事:
It's none of my business.

3. 太過分了:
That's too much.

That's over the top.

You're away too far

4. 別給我來這招:
Don't give me your shit.

5. 你以為你是誰?:
Who do you think you are?

Who do you think you're talking to?

Unit THIRTEEN
我討厭你！

I hate you!

我討厭你！

I detest you!

我恨你！

當有人對我們做出不好的事，或是我們想表示對對方極度的厭惡，沒有什麼比一句 I hate you! (我討厭你！)來得更清楚明白的了。

急用會話

DAISY David, how could you take my money without asking me.

大衛，你怎麼可以沒有問我就拿我的錢？

I'm telling you for the last time! It is really rude!

我再跟你講最後一遍！這樣很沒禮貌！

DAVID Stop nagging me! I just needed money then.

別嘮叨！我當時就是需要錢。

DAISY How can you say that? I hate you!

你怎麼可以這樣說？我討厭你！

180

臨 時 用 語

1. 你對我什麼都不是:
You're nothing to me.

2. 你敢！:
How dare you!

3. 臉皮真厚:
You have a lot of nerve.

4. 我永遠都不會饒恕你！:
I'll never forgive you!

你是個混球/雜種/婊子:
You're a jerk / bastard / bitch! (非常不正式)

5. 你真讓我噁心！:
You make me sick!

6. 他媽的！:
Damn it.

7. 放手:
Let go.

今天我很不對勁

英文補給站

 Track 1-6-14

Today is not my day.

今天我很不對勁。

It's not my day today.

我今天很衰。

天有不測風雲，當度過一個意外連連的一天，我們可以跟旁人說Today is not my day.(今天正不是我的日子啊)，來表示心中無奈與不對勁的心情。

急用會話

TOM Today is not my day!

今天我很不對勁。

TINA Oh, dear. Why do you say that?

喔，親愛的，為什麼你這麼說？

TOM First, I got up late this morning and then I lost my wallet this afternoon.

首先，我今天早上遲了些才起床，然後我今天下午又丟了錢包。

TINA Poor you!

真是個可憐的傢伙！

臨 時 用 語

1. 可憐的傢伙：

Poor guy.

2. 我今天很衰：

I am unlucky today.

I am unfortunate today.

3. 這是難免的事：

It happens!

4. 太不公平了：

It's unfair.

5. 別怕！：

Don't panic!

6. 你看上去心虛：

You look guilty.

7. 你這膽小鬼：

You are a chicken.

我很厭倦工作

英文補給站

 Track 1-6-15

I am sick of working.

我很厭倦工作。

She is tired of her job.

她厭倦了她的工作。

This job sucks!

這工作爛透了!

本章的句子可用於表達對某件事物厭倦,不耐的心情。要注意的是suck(糟糕)這一個字十分口語化跟不禮貌,切記勿在正式場合使用。

急用會話

FRANK How are you? You look terrible!

你好嗎?你看起來很糟。

SANDY I feel really fatigued.

我覺得好累。

I am really sick of working all day long.

整日工作使我厭煩。

FRANK Poor you.

可憐。

臨 時 用 語

1. 我都膩了：
I'm fed up.

2. 真讓我失望：
I'm very disappointed.

3. 這就是人生：
That's life!

2. 生活並不總是甜蜜的：
Life is not always sweet.

3. 這真是愚蠢：
That's stupid.

What a stupid idiot!

4. 爛透了：
That sucks!

Look at this mess!

5. 我們完了！：
We're through.

NOTE BOOK

Ladies and gentlemen, welcome to our hotel, where you
Do you need any help?
I need some vegetables and
Many students like to stay at home
How about coming with us
It is a coincidence that my bir

哈啦最急用 Joining in the Conversation

第七章

臨時
急用

道別
Chapter Seven Saying Goodbye

e vegeta
students like to stay at home
coming with us?
that my birthday is the same as hers

Unit ONE

再見！

 Track 1-7-01

Goodbye!

再見！

See you!

再見！

See you tomorrow.

明天見！

一般朋友之間的道別，我們可以用最常聽的
Bye!或者是See you!就可以了。

JUDY Finally! I have finished all my work.

終於，我把工作做完了！

I am going home now. Goodbye!

我要回家了，掰掰。

KELVIN See you tomorrow!

明天見。

臨 時 用 語

1. 再見:

See you soon.

See you next time.

Ciao.

(Ciao原為義大利文的問候語,現已普遍使用來
表示再見)

2. 待會兒見:

(下列句子可應用在如果只是離開不久,一會兒
就要見面的情況。)

See you around.

See you later.

Later.

單 字 解 說

1. soon 副詞:(時間)很快地

例 Please reply to my letter as soon as possible.

請儘快回覆我的信件。

2. later 副詞:(時間)稍後地

例 What you order will come later.

你訂的東西等一下會來。

Unit Two
不好意思，我要走了

Excuse me, I am about to leave.
不好意思，我要走了。

Let's go.
我們走吧！

Let's get together again.
改天再聚聚。

除了Bye-Bye，我們還可以用我要離開了，或是改天再聚來表示告別。所以，當聽到對方跟你說 "Let's get together again"，可別讀不懂空氣，而繼續待在原地不動喔。

急用會話

GINA It's very nice to talk to you today.
很高興今天能跟你聊天。

I am about to leave.
我要走了。

Let's get together again.
我們改天再聚聚。

GARY OK, good-bye.
好啊，再見。

臨 時 用 語

1. 我要走了:

I have to go now!

2. 你可以走了:

You may leave now.

(英國人士常用本句來委婉地表示自己要離開了。)

3. 下次再聊:

Catch up with you later.

Catch you later.

4. 謝謝你的款待:

Thanks for having me.

單 字 解 說

1. catch up with 動詞:片語追趕上

例 I have to study harder to catch up with my classmates.

我要再努力一點才能趕上我同學的進度。

(catch up with 原意就是追趕上某人的進度或者是程度,因此在口語中,則常被應用表示為跟對方聊天,以追趕上對方目前的狀況。)

Unit THREE

請您替我向府上各位問好！

Please give my best regards to your family.

請您替我向府上各位問好！

Give my best to John.

幫我跟約翰問聲好。

Have a nice weekend!

祝你周末愉快。

在與人道別的時候，除了 Bye-bye (再見) 之外，如果能再多加些問候的話語，會讓關係更親密。

急用會話

PATTY It's very lovely to have a chat with you.

跟你聊天真的很好。

But it is about time to leave. Sorry, but see you around.

但是我該走了。抱歉，再見囉。

PETER Good-bye. Please give my best regards to your family.

掰掰。請您替我向府上各位問好！

PATTY Thank you.

192

謝謝。

臨 時 用 語

1. 請代我向你母親問好:

Please say hello to your mother for me.

2. 幫我跟他問好:

Say hi to him for me.

3. 祝好運:

Good luck.

4. 祝好:

Have a nice day.

5. 祝周末愉快:

Have a nice weekend.

單 字 解 說

1. chat 名詞:聊天

例 It is impolite to chat in a meeting.

在會議中聊天是一件不禮貌的事。

保持聯絡!

英文補給站

 Track 1-7-04

Keep in touch.
保持聯繫。
Call me.
再打電話給我喔!
So long.
再見

與人道別,如果是長時間的分開,我們會說
Keep in touch來提醒彼此,保持聯絡。而So
long雖也是再見之意,但是有永別的意思,會
在文章或是歌詞見到,一般生活會話裡比較不
常聽到。

急用會話

MIKE I have to go to the boarding gate.
我必須要去登機門了。
Let's keep in touch.
讓我們保持聯繫吧。
MICHELLE Of course. Don't forget to call
me!
當然,別忘了打電話給我喔!

臨 時 用 語

1. 保持聯絡：
Stay in touch.
Keep in contact.

2. 別忘了我們：
Don't forget us.

3. 保重：
Take care!
Take care of yourself.

4. 再見(永別)：
So long for now.
Farewell.

5. 希望能很快見到你：
I hope to see you again soon.

單 字 解 說

1. gate 名詞：大門

例 Every morning, our principal always greets us in front of the school gate.
每天早上校長都在校門口迎接我們。

NOTE BOOK

哈啦最急用 Joining in the Conversation

第八章

電話英文
Chapter Eight Telephone English

𝓤nit ONE
嗨，我是艾咪

Track 1-8-01

Hello, this is Amy.
嗨，我是艾咪。
This is Amy speaking.
我是艾咪。
May I ask who's calling, please?
請問是誰打來的?

一般而言，我們常在電話裡以自我介紹開始電話交談。而這時候會以 "This is＿＿＿." 開頭。如果你在接電話的時候對方沒有表明他是誰，你可以問說 "May I ask who's calling, please?" (請問是誰打來的?)。

急用會話

TOM Hello.
嗨。
AMY Hello, this is Amy.
嗨，我是艾咪。
TOM Hello, this is Tom speaking.
嗨，我是湯姆。

198

臨 時 用 語

1. 我可以跟約翰說話嗎?:

May I speak to John, please?

(如果你打電話給特定的某個人,那麼你得用禮貌的問句來表達意圖)

2. 我是Carlos,我可以和Lisa說話嗎?:

This is Carlos. Could I speak to Lisa, please?

3. 你是誰?:

Who's speaking?

May I have your name, please?

And you are?

You are...?

4. 這是約翰,你請說吧:

This is John. Go ahead.

5. 請說:

Go ahead, sir.

Keep going.

𝖀nit Two
請先別掛斷，稍等一下

英文補給站 Track 1-8-02

Please hold.
請先別掛斷，稍等一下。
Hold on.
稍等一下。
Can I have extension 123?
我要找分機123。

在電話中，"Please hold" 是表示"等一下"。當你需要transferred（轉接）到另一台分機 (extension)，你會常聽到"Please hold, I'll transfer you."。

急用會話

OPERATOR Hello, Slim Yoga, How can I help you?
健美瑜珈公司您好，我能幫您嗎？
GINA This is Gina Smith. Can I have extension 123?
我是吉娜史密斯，能幫我轉分機123嗎？
OPERATOR Of course, hold on a minute, I'll put you through to extension 123.
沒問題，請等一下！我將為您轉接分機123。

200

臨 時 用 語

1. 請稍後，不要掛斷：

Please hold the line.

Hang on and wait, please.

One moment, please.

Just a minute, please.

Wait a moment.

(如果你是在繁忙時段撥打某公司電話，在接線員將你轉到另一條線之前，你可能會聽到簡短的一句話："Connecting your call..."或"，"Hello, please hold!")

2. 我是接線生，我可以提供什麼協助？：

Operator, may I help you?

3. 我幫你轉接電話：

I will transfer your call.

I will connect you.

I will redirect your call.

4. 可以幫我轉你主管嗎？：

Can you transfer my call to your supervisor?

Unit THREE

他不在，我能幫您留言給他嗎？

 Track 1-8-03

> He is not here. Can I take a message for him?
> 他不在，我能幫您留言給他嗎？
> Would you leave a message?
> 你要留言嗎？

當你打電話的對象不在或不能接聽電話時，準備好留言。如果你正在和總機講話，他們會問 Would you like to leave a message?(你要留言嗎?)，或是你可以說，May I leave a message? (我可以留言嗎?)。

急用會話

KELVIN Hello, this is Kelvin. Could I speak to Leo?
嗨，我是凱爾文，我要找里歐。

LINDA He is not in. Can I take a message for him?
他不在喔。我能幫您留言給他嗎？

KELVIN No, thanks. I'll call later.
沒關係，謝謝，我待會兒在打給他。

> **LINDA** OK, Bye-Bye.
> 好啊,再見。

臨 時 用 語

1. 他不在:
He is not available.
He is unavailable.
He is not around.

2. 他正在忙:
He is busy.

3. 你要他回電嗎?:
Would you like him to call you back?

4. 你要留言嗎?:
Would you like to leave a message?
Any message?

*記得要有禮貌

在電話中禮貌是很重要的。當你詢問事情時
用一些慣用語,如, "Could you" , "Would
you" ,及 "Please" 。然後結束對話完後記得
常常說 "Thank you" 和 "Goodbye" !

Unit FOUR
我會請他回電

 Track 1-8-04

I will have him call you back.
我會請他回電。
Can I call back later?
我可以等一下再打來嗎?
I will try again later.
我等下再打來。

當你打電話,而對方正在忙或者是不在時,你可以說Can I call back later?(我可以等一下再打來嗎?)。

急用會話

TOM Hello, Tina? This is Tom.
嗨,堤娜?我是湯姆。

SANDY This is Sandy. I will get her. Just a minute please.
我是珊蒂。我去叫她,你請等一下。

SANDY She is not around, but I will have her call you back.
她不在,我會叫她回電給你。

TOM Thank you.
謝謝。

1. 你可以過幾分鐘再打來看看：

You can try again in a few minutes.

2. 你介意等一下再打電話過來嗎？：

Would you mind calling me back later?

3. 她正在忙線中：

She is on another line.

4. 轉告他我有打電話過來：

Please tell him I called.

5. 我會回電：

I will return the call.

6. 我該什麼時候回電？：

When should I call back?

7. 抱歉那麼晚才來接電話：

I am sorry for the delay.

Unit FIVE
我聽不請楚

英文補給站

 Track 1-8-05

I cannot hear you very well.
我聽不請楚。
I cannot hear you.
我聽不見。

講電話或手機時,難免因為對方音量或這是收訊問題,而聽不清楚對方的聲音。為了不錯失重要訊息,一定要趕快跟對方說I cannot hear you very well. (我聽不請楚)。

急用會話

DINA This is Dina calling, is Jamie in?
這是戴安,傑咪在嗎?

ANN She is on another line at this moment. Can I take a message?
她正在另一條線上,我可以幫你留言。

DINA Yes, Could you ask her to call back at...
好啊,你可以叫她回電…。

ANN Sorry, but I cannot hear you very well.
抱歉,我聽不請楚。

DINA Well, I will try again later.

好吧，我會再回撥。

1. 你在說什麼?:
What?

What are you saying?

2. 可不可以再大聲一點?:
Louder, please.

Can you speak louder?

3. 可不可以說慢一點?:
Slower, please.

Please speak slowly.

(在電話中，如果你不確定你是否能聽懂所有的
英語對話，一定要坦承。直接告訴對方："My
English isn't very strong. Could you please speak
slowly?" 大部分的人都會慢下語速，來讓你聽
懂，並很高興你這麼做。)

4. 我想和詢問台連絡:
I want to talk to the information desk.

5. 請轉服務部:
Service Division, please.

我等一下再回電話給你

英文補給站

Track 1-8-06

I will call you back later.
我等一下再回電話給你。
Call you later.
再回電給你。
Talk to you later.
待會聊。

當有人來電，而你正忙著手邊的事物；或者是要在電話中道別時，我們都可以簡單的說一句 Call you later (再回電給你)。

急用會話

CATHY Did you call me?
你有打電話給我嗎？

CAESAR No, I did not call you. And I am sort of busy right now.
沒有，我沒有打電話給你。我現在有點忙。

CATHY All right. Call you later.
好吧，再回電給你。

臨 時 用 語

1. 我會回你電話:

I will return your call.

2. 我可以五分鐘之後再打來嗎?:

Could I call again in 5 minutes?

3. 能告訴她我來電過嗎?:

Can you tell her that I called?

Please tell her I called.

4. 抱歉讓你久等了:

Sorry for keeping you waiting.

I am sorry for the delay.

Thank you for waiting.

5. 很高興跟你說話:

Nice talking to you.

單 字 解 說

1. missed call 名詞：未接來電

𝕌nit SEVEN
抱歉，我真的不能再説了

Sorry, I must end the conversation.
抱歉，我不能再説了。
Sorry, I've got to hang up.
抱歉，我得掛電話了。
Shall we continue this later?
我們可不可以晚一點再繼續談？

有人喜歡講電話講到天長地久，但是我們總是
有時候有急事需要掛電話。這時候，我們就可
以跟電話那一頭的對方説，Sorry, I must end
the conversation.(抱歉，我不能再説了)。

急用會話

JIM Sorry, I must end the conversation.
抱歉，我不能再説了。
There's someone on the other line.
另一線有人找。
JOAN That's OK. It's nice to have a talk
with you today.
好吧。不過今天真高興能跟你説話。
JIM Bye. I'll talk to you later.
再見。我晚點再打給你。

1. 我得掛電話了：

I've really got to go.

2. 我想我該讓你去忙了：

I think I'd better let you go.

3. 我老婆在等我：

My wife's waiting for me.

4. 我要回去工作了：

I have to get back to work.

5. 我不耽誤你時間了：

I won't keep you any longer.

6. 我有插播：

I've got a call waiting.

7. 有點晚了。我們何不明天再談呢？：

It's kind of late. Why don't we talk
about it tomorrow?

(以上幾句非常適合用於我們要禮貌性地終止電
話對話。)

ⓊⓃⒾⓉ Eight
告訴他儘快回我電話

Track 1-8-08

Please tell him to return my call ASAP.
告訴他儘快回我電話。
Have him call me at 777.
請他回撥777給我。

當我們有急事找人，卻打電話找不到人，我們
說Please tell him to return my call ASAP (告訴
他儘快回我電話)以留言請人儘快請對方回電。

STEVE This is Steve speaking. I want to
speak to your manager.
我是史蒂夫，我要跟你們經理說話。
OPERATOR The manager is not at his
desk.
經理現在不在座位上。
STEVE Please tell him to return my call
at 777 ASAP.
請他儘快回我電話777。
It is urgent!
有急事！

212

臨 時 用 語

1. 請問你的電話號碼?:

Your number, please?

Does he have your phone number?

2. 我會轉告他的:

I will let him know.

I will have him call you back.

3. 我需要跟他說話:

I need to talk to him.

4. 他要怎麼跟你聯絡?:

How can he get a hold of you?

5. 我要找分機503:

Could I have extension number 503?

Can I have extension 503 please?

(用於當你只知道分機號碼卻不知道人名的時候)

單 字 解 說

1. ASAP = as soon as possible 儘快

Unit NINE
你打錯了

Wrong number.
你打錯了。
I'm afraid you got the wrong number.
你打錯了。
Sorry, I think you have the wrong number.
你打錯了。

誤撥電話號碼，我們可以跟人家說一聲Sorry
(抱歉)；如果接到人家打錯電話，我們可以說
Sorry, but wrong number. (抱歉，你打錯了)來
告知對方。

急用會話

FRANK May I speak to Graham, please?
我要跟格蘭說話。

JEAN There is no Graham here.
這裡沒有叫格蘭的人。

I'm afraid you have the wrong number.
我想你打錯了喔。

214

臨 時 用 語

1. 你撥幾號?:

What number are you dialling?

What number are you trying to reach?

2. 您撥的電話是空號:

The number you have reached is not in service.

3. 忙線中:

The line is busy.

4. 歡迎隨時來電:

Please feel free to call.

Call me whenever you want.

單 字 解 說

1. afraid 形容詞:害怕的

例 I am afraid of the dark.

我怕黑。

2. dial 動詞:撥(電話號碼)

例 Can I dial directly?

我可以直接撥嗎?

Unit TEN

哪裡有公共電話？

英文補給站

Track 1-8-10

Where's the pay phone?
哪裡有公共電話？
Is there a pay phone?
這有公共電話嗎？
I need to make a call.
我需要打通電話。

出門在外，難免遇到忘記帶手機，或者是手機沒電的時候，這時候我們可以問路人一句 Where's the pay phone? (哪裡有公共電話？) 來應急。

急用會話

STACY Where is the pay phone?
哪裡有公共電話？
I need to make a call.
我需要打通電話。
NELSON It's just across the street. See, it's over there.
就在對街。看！就在那兒。
STACY Thank you.
謝謝。

216

臨 時 用 語

1. 請問有公共電話嗎？：

Is there a public phone?

I'm looking for the phone booth.

2. 我可以跟你借用手機嗎?：

May I use your cell phone?

3. 我想打長途電話：

I want to make a long distance call.

How do I call long distance?

4. 打電話到台灣要多少錢？：

What's the rate to Taiwan?

單 字 解 說

1. public phone/ pay phone 公共電話
2. phone booth 電話亭
3. cell phone/ mobile phone 手機
4. smart phone 智慧型手機

對不起這麼晚打電話來

英文補給站

Track 1-8-11

I'm sorry to call you so late.
對不起這麼晚打電話來。
I'm sorry to bother you at this hour.
很抱歉在這時打擾你。

太早，或太晚打電話給對方，我們通常會在通話一開始就表達我們的歉意，除了Sorry，更完整的說法是I'm sorry to call you so late. (對不起這麼晚打電話來)。

急用會話

TELEPHONE ANSWERING MACHINE This is a recording.
這是電話答錄機。
I'm not at home now. Please leave a message after the beep. Thank you.
我現在不在家，請在嗶的一聲之後開始留言。謝謝！
KEN This is Ken. I'm sorry to call you so late.
我是肯。對不起這麼晚打電話來。
Please phone me back at 2783-6655.
請回電2783-6655。

臨 時 用 語

1. 電話號碼英文講法：

區域號碼：area code

電話號碼：02-2783-6655

唸成 area code zero-two, two-seven-eight-three-six-six-five-five.

(0 可念成 oh 或 zero，而 66 可念成 six-six 或 double six)

2. 在英文中，對電話答錄機留話時內容與中文一般留言無異，說出以下重點即可：姓名，目的，回電號碼。

例 This is Kathy. Please give me a call when you are free. My call back number is 2908-3426.

我是凱西。有空請回電。我的回電號碼是2908-3426。

單 字 解 說

1. answering machine 名詞：電話答錄機

(類似的說法有：voicemail電子錄音系統)

2. call back number 名詞：回電號碼

NOTE
BOOK

Ladies and gentlemen, welcome to our hotel, where yo
Do you need any help?
I need some vegetables and
Many students like to stay at home
How about coming with u
It is a coincidence that my bir

國外旅行最急用 In Travelling

第一章

問路
Chapter One Asking for Directions

ne vegetab
students like to stay at hom
coming with us?
that my birthday is the same as hers.

火車站在哪裡?

英文補給站

Track 2-1-01

Where is the central station?
火車站在哪裡?
How do I get to the central station?
火車站在哪裡?
Where are you going?
你要去哪裡?

國外旅遊,在一個城市裡,常常會以當地的 central station (火車站,你也可以說train station)為出發中心。所以,一旦迷路,或要搭車時,別忘了隨口問人一句, Where is the central station? (火車站在哪裡?)喔。

急用會話

JESSICA Excuse me.
不好意思。
Where is the central station?
火車站在哪裡?
ANDREW You just go straight.
你就直走。
You will see it on your right hand side.
你就會看到它在你的右手邊。

臨 時 用 語

1. 表明方位常用英文單詞

東: east　西: west　南: south　北: north

左: left　右: right　前: front　後: back

往前: straight

在右邊. on the right

在左邊: on the left

轉右邊: turn right

轉左邊: turn left

直走: go straight

這邊: here

那邊: there

2. 常詢問地點:

機場: airport

公車站: bus station/bus stop

地鐵站:

metro station (歐洲常用)

subway station(美國常用)

underground(英國常用)

飯店旅館: hotel

遊客中心: Information center

Unit Two

這附近有遊客資訊中心嗎?

Track 2-1-02

Is there any information center?
這附近有遊客資訊中心嗎?
Is there any information center around?
這附近有遊客資訊中心嗎?
Where is the nearest metro station?
最近的地鐵站在哪?

除了像前一章用where(哪裡)和how(如何)直接問
你要去的地方怎麼走之外,我們也可以換一種
說法,Is there any information center? (這附近
有遊客資訊中心嗎?)。

急用會話

BETTY Hello, I am a tourist.
嗨,我是遊客。
Is there any information center?
這附近有遊客資訊中心嗎?
GINO It's just around the corner.
它就在轉角處。

224

臨 時 用 語

1. 常詢問地點:

銀行: bank　酒吧: bar　咖啡館: caf'e

外幣兌換中心: change bureau

藥房: pharmacy/ drug store

餐廳: restaurant

醫院: hospital

公共廁所: public toilet

郵局: post office

電話亭: phone booth

警局: police office

百貨公司: department store

夜店: night club

2. 到旅館遠嗎?:

How far is it to a hotel?

Is a hotel far?

Am I near a hotel?

Am I close to a hotel?

Is a hotel nearby?

單 字 解 說

1. corner 名詞：角落；轉角
2. nearby 副詞：附近

這是去博物館的近路嗎?

英文補給站 Track 2-1-03

Is this the shortcut to the museum?
這是去博物館地近路嗎?
What's the quickest way to the gallery?
哪一條是去畫廊的近路?

走的很累,而想問人哪一條路是近路時,可以說Is this the shortcut to the museum? (這是去博物館地近路嗎?)。如果身上剛好有地圖,也可以直接拿著地圖問人說,Where am I? (我在哪兒?)。

急用會話

LISA Excuse me. Where is No.5 Street?
對不起,第五大街在哪兒?
PETER Where are you going?
你要去哪?
LISA I am going to the museum there.
我要去那兒的博物館。
Is this the shortcut to the museum?
這是去博物館地近路嗎?
PETER Sorry, but I do not know.
抱歉,我不知道。

臨 時 用 語

1. 哪一條路最快?:

Which is the fastest way?

2. （打開地圖）我在哪兒?:

Where am I?

Where am I on this map?

Can you point out where I am on the map?

Please show me where I am.

3. 我在哪條街上?:

What's the name of the street?

What street am I on?

單 字 解 說

1. map 名詞：地圖
2. museum 名詞：博物館
3. gallery 名詞：畫廊

Unit FOUR
我迷路了

I am lost.
我迷路了。

I don't know where I am.
我迷路了。

真的不幸在陌生的地方迷路了,一定要大膽地為自己說一句,I am lost. Can you show the direction? (我迷路了,你能幫我指路嗎?)。

急用會話

SEAN Excuse me, but I am lost.
抱歉,但我迷路了。

Can you give me directions?
你能幫我指路嗎?

FRED Of course. Where to?
當然,去哪?

SEAN City Gallery.
市立畫廊。

FRED That way. It's just around the corner.
那個方向,轉彎就是。

臨 時 用 語

1. 我要去市立畫廊:

I am going to City Gallery.

I want to go to City Gallery.

I would like to go to City Gallery.

2. 指引方位英文常用句:

走出這個餐廳: go out of the restaurant

穿越這條街: go through the street.

經過超商: go past the supermarket

再繼續走: keep walking

左轉: turn left

右轉: turn right

走到這條路的盡頭:

go to the end of the road

市立畫廊在你的右手邊:

City Gallery is on your right.

Unit FIVE
感謝你為我指路

英文補給站

 Track 2-1-05

Thank you for directions.
感謝你為我指路。
You can get there on foot.
你能用走的到那邊。
You can't miss it.
你不可能看錯的。

當別人為我們指路或帶路之後，我們一定別忘了要說一句Thank you for directions. (感謝你為我指路)，來表示我們的感謝之情。

急用會話

WINNIE The coffee shop is next to the City Hall.
那個咖啡店就在市政廳的旁邊。
You will walk along the road until you hit the first traffic light.
你要沿著路走，直到你遇到第一個紅綠燈。
You will see it at the corner on your right.
你會看到它就在你右邊的轉角處。
DEAN Thank you for the directions.

感謝你為我指路。

臨 時 用 語

1. 就在市政廳的旁邊：

It's beside the City Hall.

2. 就在市政廳的對面：

It is across from the City Hall.

It is opposite the City Hall.

It's on the opposite side of the City Hall.

It faces the City Hall.

2. 就在博物館跟市政廳的中間：

It's between the museum and the City Hall.

單 字 解 說

1. traffic light 名詞：紅綠燈
2. crossing 名詞：十字路口
3. block 名詞：街區
4. direction 名詞：指引方向

Unit Six
我怎麼坐車去臺北?

 Track 2-1-06

How can I get to Taipei by train?
我怎麼坐火車去臺北?
Which line should I take to go to Paris?
去巴黎應該乘座哪條線?

出國自助旅行，搭乘大眾交通工具是一定要的啦！所以，本單元介紹搭火車(train)/電車(tramp)問站問路英文。

急用會話

DAVE How can I get to Tokyo by train?
我怎麼坐火車去東京?

PASSER-BY 1 You can get a map and ask for more detailed information at the Information Center.
你可以在詢問處拿到地圖以及得到更多資訊。

PASSER-BY 2 You can take the Yamancte line. It's a green train.
你可以乘坐山手線，是綠色的火車。

232

臨 時 用 語

1. 下一站是哪？：

What's the next station?

2. 下站是約克：

The next station is York station.

3. 到紐約有多少個站？：

How many stops are there to New York?

4. 你在哪下車？：

Where do you get off?

5. 你可以在到的時候告訴我嗎？

Would you tell me when I get there?

6. 那是第四個站：

That's the fourth stop.

7. 你可以在第二站下：

You can get off at the second stop.

離這裡有多少站啊？

英文補給站

 Track 2-1-07

Where can I get on a subway to the zoo?
在哪裡可以坐到動物園的地鐵？
Is this the right bus to the zoo?
這是去動物園的公車嗎？
How many stops is it from here?
離這裡有多少站啊？

除了火車電車，公車、地鐵也是另一種常見的
大眾運輸系統。本單元介紹搭公車(bus)/地鐵
(subway/underground/MRT)問站問路英文。

急用會話

STEVE Is this the right bus to the zoo?
這是去動物園的公車嗎？
FANNY Yes.
是啊。
STEVE How many stops is it from here?
離這裡有多少站啊？
FANNY That's the 5th stop.
那是第五站。

1. 這是去動物園的公車/地鐵嗎?:

Does this bus/subway go to the zoo?

Does this bus/subway stop at Taipei
Station?

Which bus/subway could I get on to
Taipei?

Is it for the zoo?

2. 下一個公車站在哪?:

Where is the next bus station?

3. 我要在哪兒下車?:

Where can I get off?

4. 你要乘哪一條地鐵?:

Which subway are you taking?

5. (地鐵)的出口在街道的拐角:

The exit is on the corner of the street.

6. 從M8出口出去:

Take Exit M8.

ᘔnit Eight
火車什麼時候開?

 Track 2-1-08

When will the train depart?
火車什麼時候開?
Will we depart on time?
我們會準時出發嗎?
How long is the ride?
車程多久?

找到了你要乘坐的公車,火車或是地鐵,車什麼時候開(When will the train depart?),要做多久(How long is the ride?),都是一般旅人關心的問題。如有疑問,就大膽的問一下身旁路人(passer-by)或者是櫃檯(information desk)的服務人員吧!

急用會話

HENRY I am going to the City Hall.
我要去市政府。
When will the train depart?
火車什麼時候開?
TOM It departs at 10 o'clock.
十點開車。

臨 時 用 語

1. 公車多久來一次?:
How often do the buses run?

2. 這班火車要在第幾月台搭?:
Which platform is the train on?

3. 在第11月台:
It's on the platform 11.

4. 火車三點發車:
The train will depart at 3 o'clock.

5. 這班火車誤點了:
This train is delayed.

6. 到那要坐多久?:
How long does this bus trip take?
How long does it take to get there?

7. 我什麼時候可以到市政府?:
When will I reach the City Hall?
When can I get to the City Hall?

英文補給站

 Track 2-1-09

Where's the taxi stand?
計程車站在哪裡？

Where can I get a taxi?
在哪裏能乘到計程車？

A taxi, please.
幫我叫輛計程車。

預算高一點，或者是真的趕時間，我們會選擇搭乘計程車(taxi/cab)。國外的計程車常常是有固定的招呼點，如果我們要搭車，也是要向人詢問 Where's the taxi stand？(計程車站在哪裏？)。

急用會話

ASHLEY Where's the taxi stand?
計程車站在哪？

JEFF You can walk along the street and you will see it on your right.
你可沿著這條街走，然後你會在右手邊看到它。

Or you can call 25671818 to hail a taxi cab.
或者是你可以打 25671818 來招一台計程

車。

臨 時 用 語

1. 要載嗎？：
May I?

2. 需要搭計程車嗎?：
Are you looking for a taxi?

3. 我可以送你過去：
I can take you there.

4. 我可以送你一程：
I can give you a ride.

5. 我要在哪放你下來?：
Where can I drop you?

單 字 解 說

1. stand 名詞：小攤子

2. hail 動詞：招呼 hail a taxi 招呼計程車。

3. ride 名詞：車程

Unit TEN
你要去哪裡?

Where would you like to go to?
你要去哪裡?

To the airport, please.
請到機場。

To this place, please.
請載我到這裡。

坐上計程車,除非車上提供中文服務,不然跟司機講幾句英文溝通價錢跟目的地是必要的。本單元介紹計程車上對話常用急救英文。

急用會話

RICHARD Where would you like to go to?
你要去哪裡?

BRIAN To the airport, please.
請到機場。

(這時候,如果要去的地方不會用英文說,我們可以攤開地圖,或是把事先寫好的地址給司機說To this place, please.)

臨 時 用 語

1. 你要去哪?:

Where to?

2. 請帶我去機場:

Drive me to the airport, please.

Please take me to the airport.

I want to go to the airport.

3. 請帶我去這個地址:

Please take me to the address on it.

4. 麻煩這裡停:

Stop here, please.

5. 麻煩在這裡等一下:

Wait here, please.

6. 我要在這裡下車:

Let me off here, please.

Unit ELEVEN
車資多少?

 Track 2-1-11

How much?
車資多少?
How much is the fare?
車資多少?
How much do I owe you?
車資多少?

在計程車上,除了與司機閒話家常。重點在於要下計程車付車資時,也得會說幾句車資議價的英文。本單元介紹計程車上對話常用英文。

急用會話

MARVIN I'll get off here. Thank you.
How much?
我要這裡下車。謝謝。車資多少?

DRIVER 98 dollars, please.
請付98元。

MARVIN Thank you so much indeed.
Please keep the change.
真的太謝謝您了。不用找了。

1. 你能開快點嗎？我趕時間:

Could you please drive faster? I'm in a hurry.

2. 你能開一下車窗嗎？:

Could you open the window?

3. 你能開一下音響嗎?:

Please turn on the radio.

4. 禁止吸菸:

No smoking.

Smoking is not allowed.

5. 別忘了你的隨身物品:

Don't forget your belongings.

6. 我們到了:

Here we are.

Unit TWELVE
租一台車多少錢?

 Track 2-1-12

How much is it to rent a car?

租一台車多少錢?

How much does it cost to rent a SUV?

租一台休旅車多少錢?

三兩好友外出旅遊,如果我們有駕照(driver's license),又會開車,有時候租車(rent a car)也是不錯的選擇。本單元介紹租車對話常用英文。

ANDY How much is it to rent a car?

租一台車多少錢?

CLERK $20.00 a day.

一天二十美金。

ANDY Could I have one for tomorrow?

我可以租一台明天用嗎?

CLERK Sure. Your driver's license, please.

當然可以啊。你有駕照嗎?

ANDY Here you are.

在這。

244

臨 時 用 語

1. 租一台車多少錢?:

What's the rate for a car?

If I want to rent a car, how much will it cost?

2. 你有駕照嗎?:

Your driver's license, please.

Do you have your driver's license?

Can I see your license, please?

May I see your driver's license?

3. 我要租一台周日用:

I would like to reserve one for this Sunday.

4. 請付50元押金:

Please leave a $50 deposit.

5. 請填一下表格:

Complete this form.

Fill out this form, please.

Unit THIRTEEN
能讓我搭便車嗎?

 Track 2-1-13

Can you please give me a lift?
能讓我搭便車嗎?
Do you need a ride?
你需要搭便車嗎?
Need a free ride?
你需要搭便車嗎?

到國外,一時之間迷了路,又找不到大眾交通工具(mass transportation/ public transportation),我們可以嘗試搭便車。除了伸出大拇指招車之外,我們還可以問人一句,Can you please give me a lift? (能讓我搭便車嗎?)。

急用會話

VIVIAN Excuse me. I want to go downtown.
不好意思。我要去市區。
Can you please give me a lift?
能讓我搭便車嗎?
ADAM Sure. Hop on in.
好啊,上車吧!

臨 時 用 語

1. 我搭便車到機場:

I hitched a ride to the airport.

Someone gave me a lift to the airport.

Someone offered me a free ride to the airport.

2. 我可以載你一程:

I can give you a lift.

3. 上車:

Get in.

You may get in.

4. 開車小心:

Drive safe.

5. 請在這個轉角讓我下車:

Please drop me at this corner.

Please let me off at this corner.

單 字 解 說

1. 搭便車: hitch a ride

2. 搭便車的人: hitchhiker

NOTE
BOOK

國外旅行最急用 In Travelling

第二章

臨時急用

問時間
Chapter Two Asking for the Time

Unit ONE

現在幾點?

  Track 2-2-01

What time is it?
現在幾點?

Do you have the time?
現在幾點?

What time?
幾點?

當我們到了機場、火車站或遊樂園卻沒有戴手表,不知道時間時,我們可以問一下路人,What time is it, please? (請問現在幾點?)。或者,有人要邀約你出遊時,你也可以先問What time?(幾點?),來確認約會時間。

GINA Excuse me.
不好意思。

What time is it, please?
請問現在幾點?

ROBERT It's three o'clock.
現在三點囉。

250

臨 時 用 語

1. 你的錶幾點了？：

What's the time by your watch?

2. 你幾點抵達？：

What time do you arrive?

3. 你幾點離開？：

What time do you leave?

4. 現在是四點一刻：

It's a quarter past four.

5. 現在差十分五點：

It's ten minutes to five.

6. 現在是七點半：

It's half past seven.

7. 現在三點整：

It's three o'clock sharp.

時間緊迫!

英文補給站

 Track 2-2-02

Hurry up!
時間緊迫!

I am in a hurry.
我在趕時間。

I have to hurry away.
我想我要趕快走了。

一群人出遊,難免拖拖拉拉。為了提醒大家時間,我們可以大喊,Hurry up! (時間緊迫!動作快!)。

急用會話

NINA We have to arrive at the theater at two o'clock.
我們要在兩點到戲院。

Now, it is ten minutes to two.
現在在十分鐘就要兩點了。

Hurry up.
動作快啊!

臨 時 用 語

1. 我現在很趕:
I am in a rush.

2. 大家動起來啊:
Let's move.

3. 只剩三分鐘了:
There are only three minutes left.

Three minutes left.

4. 我們必須準時到那裡:
We have to arrive there on time.

5. 你能提早到嗎?:
Can you arrive earlier?

Can you come here ahead of time?

6. 我的錶快十分鐘:
My watch is ten minutes fast.

𝔘nit THREE
太遲了

It is too late.

太遲了。

We are late.

我們遲到了。

It's still early.

還早。

當我們發現預定的時間過了，我們就是遲到了
(We are late.)。如果是提早到，那就還早(It's
still early.)。

急用會話

DEREK It is a quarter past four.

現在四點十五分了。

We should arrive at the airport at four.

我們應該在四點就到該到機場。

We are terribly late.

我們一整個大遲到。

臨 時 用 語

1. **抱歉我遲到了：**

I am sorry for being late.

2. **我今天早上上班遲到：**

I was late for work this morning.

3. **我今晚的晚會提早到：**

I will be early for the party tonight.

4. **火車會晚點開：**

The train is delayed.

5. **活動延期了：**

The activity is put off.

單 字 解 說

1. late 形容詞：晚的；遲到的
2. early 形容詞：早的
3. delay 動詞：拖延；延誤

例 The car accident delayed the train for one hour.

這個車禍延誤了火車一小時。

英文補給站

Track 2-2-04

Time's up.

時間到了。

It's about time.

時間到了。

Time is running out.

時間快到了。

當我們在參與計時活動時，時間到我們會聽到人家跟我們說Time's up.。此外，在到預定要離開的時間快要到時，我們也常會說It's about time. (時間到了)或者是Time to go. (該走了)。

急用會話

JULIET I am happy to have a chat with you.

我很高興跟你聊天。

It's about time to leave.

該是我要離開的時候了

Please feel free to call.

歡迎來電啊。

RONAN Of course. Bye.

當然，掰掰。

臨 時 用 語

1. 該是睡覺的時候：

Time for bed.

It is about time to sleep.

2. 該是吃晚飯的時候：

Time for dinner.

It is about time to have dinner.

3. 我們一起倒數計時吧：

Let's count down.

4. 我們沒時間了：

We don't have time.

We have no time left.

5. 沒時間了：

There is no time.

6. 這件事要花時間：

This takes time.

7. 時光飛逝：

Time flies.

NOTE BOOK

Ladies and gentlemen, welcome to our hotel, where yo

Do you need any help?

I need some vegetables and
Many students like to stay at hom

How about coming with

It is a coincidence that my bir

國外旅行最急用 In Travelling

第三章

住宿英文
Chapter Three Accommodation

Unit ONE
我要訂雙人房

 Track 2-3-01

I would like to reserve a double room.
我要訂雙人房。
Double room, please.
請給我雙人房。
Please keep my reservation.
請保留我預訂的房間。

到國外旅遊，除了路線規劃，最重要的還有安排好住宿(accommodation)。很多人喜歡在國內上網或透過電話訂房，以節省出遊時的不便。本節將介紹電話訂房時，所需的句子與單詞。

急用會話

RECEPTIONIST Hello, Happy Holiday Hotel.
您好，快樂假期旅店。
DAVID Hello, I would like to reserve a double room.
我要訂雙人房。
RECEPTIONIST Your name, please.
您的姓名。
DAVID My name is David.
我叫大衛。

臨 時 用 語

1. **房間種類英文說法:**

   單人房: single room

   雙人房: double room

   雙人房: twin room (兩張單人床)

   三人床客房: triple room

   家庭房: family room (通常是兩間房,一間
   雙人床、一間兩張單人床)

   套房: suite

2. **我要訂1月1日一個單人套房:**

   I'd like to reserve a single suite for
   January 1.

   I want to make a reservation for a
   single suite for January 1.

3. **您要先訂房嗎?:**

   Would you like to reserve a room?

   Do you want to book a room first?

4. **我要訂三晚住宿:**

   I would like to make a reservation for
   three nights.

Unit Two
套房一晚價錢是多少?

  Track 2-3-02

What's the room rate for a suite?
套房一晚價錢是多少?
What's the price of a suite?
套房一晚價錢是多少?
Does the price include breakfast?
房價是否已含早餐?

預訂房間時,最重要的就是房價(price)問題了。詢問房價,我們除了可以用How much(多少錢)來詢問,也可以清楚地說What's the room rate for a suite? (套房一晚價錢是多少?),讓對方更清楚你的需求。

急用會話

TIM What's the room rate for a suite?
套房一晚價錢是多少?
RECEPTIONIST 35 dollars per night.
每晚35元。
TIM Does the price include breakfast?
房價是否已含早餐?
RECEPTIONIST Yes.
是的。
TIM I'll take this room.

我要訂這間房間。

臨 時 用 語

1. 包括餐費嗎?:

Are there any meals included?

2. 服務費包括在內嗎？:

Is the service charge included?

3. 房內可以上網嗎?:

Is there any internet service in the room?

4. 上網要多少錢?:

How much for the Internet?

5. 是免費的嗎?:

Is it free?

6. 那太貴了。你們有沒有便宜一些的房間?:

That is too expensive. Have you got anything cheaper?

7. 隨時都有熱水供應嗎?:

Is hot water available any time?

Unit THREE
我何時可以住進來？

What time can I check in?
我何時可以住進來？
When is check-out time?
退房的時間是幾點鐘？
May I pay by my credit card.
我可以用信用卡付款嗎？

訂房或入住登記時，要先確認好入住以及退房
時間。此外，付款方式(payment)也是一件必問
的事。

急用會話

GEORGE Here is my reservation
confirmation.
這是我的訂房確認。
RECEPTIONIST Oh. A suite for two nights.
哦。一間雙人房，兩晚。
GEORGE When is check-out time?
請問退房的時間？
RECEPTIONIST Ten o'clock in the morning.
早上十點。

臨 時 用 語

1. **訂房入住常用英文字詞:**
   reservation guarantee 訂房訂金
   check-in 住宿
   check-out 退房
   check-in reservation 提前辦理住宿
   a late check-out reservation 延後退房
   cancel a reservation 取消訂房

2. **可以給我張飯店的名片嗎?:**
   May I have the hotel business card?

3. **這裡可使用信用卡/旅行支票嗎?:**
   Do you accept credit cards / traveler's checks?

4. **餐廳在那兒?:**
   Where is the dining room?

單 字 解 說

旅館常見說法:
   旅館: hotel
   小旅館: inn
   汽車旅館: motel
   度假中心: resort
   青年旅館: hostel
   別墅: villa
   民宿: B&B (bed and breakfast)

Unit FOUR
我要辦理住宿登記

 Track 2-3-04

I'd like to check in.
我要辦理住宿登記。
I need some room service.
我需要些客房服務。
I left my key in my room.
我把鑰匙留在房間裏。

入住時，如需住房服務，我們可以跟櫃台人員
(receptionist)說明。本節將介紹常見的客房服務
英文會話。

急用會話

WENDY I'd like to check in.
我要辦理住宿登記。
Can you please give me a wake-up call
at six tomorrow morning?
請在明天早上六點鐘打電話叫醒我好嗎？
RECEPTIONIST Not a problem.
沒問題。

臨 時 用 語

1. 是否可代為保管貴重物品?:

Could you keep my valuables?

2. 我需要多一條毛毯:

I need an extra blanket.

3. 我把自己鎖在外面了:

I've locked myself out.

4. 餐廳幾點開始營業?:

What time does the dining room open?

5. 早餐幾點開始供應?:

What time can I have breakfast?

6. 請送給我一壺咖啡:

Please bring me a pot of coffee.

7. 熱水不夠熱:

The hot water is not hot enough.

8. 請問要到哪裡搭機場巴士?:

Please tell me where I can take the bus
to the airport.

Unit FIVE
我們要退房

I'd like to check out.
我要退房
My bill, please.
請給我帳單。
May I put baggage here? I will pick it up at 3PM.
請問可以借放行李嗎?我大概下午3點回來拿。

本節介紹退房時常用的英文單句。

急用會話

ANN I'd like to check out. My bill, please.
我要退房。請給我帳單。

Could we have someone help us with our bags, please?
可以找個人幫我們提行李嗎?

RECEPTIONIST Certainly. I'll ring for someone to help you.
當然可以。我幫您找個人。

268

臨 時 用 語

1. 你可以幫我拿行李當大廳嗎?:

Could you bring my baggage down to
the lobby tomorrow morning?

2. 明早請將行李放在你的門口:

Please leave them outside your room
tomorrow morning.

3. 我總共有4件行李:

I have four pieces of baggage.

4. 你何時離開?:

What time are you leaving?

5. 我住的很愉快:

I enjoyed my stay.

6. 希望您在此住得愉快:

Have a pleasant stay.

7. 這是你的收據:

Here is your receipt.

Unit six

我們客滿了

英文補給站

There is no vacancy.

我們客滿了。

這幾年旅行很流行,所以訂房稍晚一點,難免會聽到櫃台人員(receptionist)說,Sorry, but there is no vacancy.(抱歉,但是我們客滿了)。

急用會話

RECEPTIONIST Good evening. May I help you?

小姐,晚安。我能為您效勞嗎?

MIMI Yes, I'd like to check in.

是的,我要入住。

RECEPTIONIST Do you have a reservation?

您有預訂房間嗎?

MIMI No.

沒有

RECEPTIONIST Just a moment, please.

請稍等。

Sorry, but we are fully booked.

抱歉,但是我們客滿了。

1. 你們還有空房嗎?:

Do you have any vacancies?

2. 你能推薦另一個旅館給我嗎?:

Could you recommend another hotel for me?

3. 我們客滿了:

We are fully booked.

We are fully occupied.

No vacancy.

4. 我們還有空房:

We have some vacant rooms.

5. 我急需要住房:

I urgently need a room.

6. 你要什麼樣的房間?:

How kind of room would you like?

NOTE
BOOK

國外旅行最急用 In Travelling

第四章

逛街購物去
Chapter Four Go Shopping

$\mathcal{U}nit$ ONE
我只是看看

  Track 2-4-01

Do you find anything you like?
找到你喜歡的嗎?
I'm just looking, thanks.
我只是看看,謝謝。
I'd like to have a look if you don't mind.
如果不介意,我想看一下。

出去玩,除了去遊樂區或這是上山下海探索自
然奇景,逛街也是一大樂趣。當我們只是去
純逛逛,而不打花錢買東西時(window shopping),我們可以跟來詢問的店員說,I'm just
looking, thanks. (我只是看看,謝謝)。

急用會話

CLERK Do you find anything you like?
找到你喜歡的嗎?
EUNICE I'm just looking, thanks.
我只是看看,謝謝。
CLERK If you need any help, please feel
free to let me know.
如果你需要幫忙,歡迎讓我知道。

臨 時 用 語

1. 你需要些什麼?:

What can I do for you?

Can I help you?

Are you being helped?

Are you being served?

Is there anybody waiting on you?

Do you need any help?

2. 我只是看看:

I'm good.

I'd just like to have a look around.

3. 店員常用稱呼用英文:

店員: clerk

女士: ma'am

先生: sir

4. 一起去逛街吧:

Let's go shopping.

Let's go check that department store.

Would you like to go shopping with me?

Unit Two
我在找一雙鞋

Track 2-4-02

Do you have a pair of shoes?
我在找一雙鞋。

I want a pair of paints.
我想買一條褲子。

Are you looking for a pair of glasses?
你在找一副眼鏡嗎?

如果逛街時,心裡已經擬定好要買的東西,到了店裡,就可以直接跟店員說,Do you have _____? (我在找_____)。這裡要注意的是,不能直接中翻英地說,Do you "sell" something?喔!

急用會話

CLERK Is there anything I can do for you, Ma'am?
我能 您做什么,女士?

BETTY Do you have a pair of shoes?
我在找一雙鞋。

CLERK This way, please.
請往這走。

276

臨 時 用 語

1. 我想找一支錶：

I'd like to see a watch.

Where can I find a watch?

I'm interested in a watch.

I want to buy a watch.

I am looking for a watch.

2. 請把那個給我看看：

Show me that one, please.

Let me have a look at that.

Would you show me that?

3. 你今天要些茶葉嗎?：

Do you want any tea today?

What about some tea?

單 字 解 說

1. a pair of 一雙；一對；一副

    用法：

    a pair of gloves (手套)

    scissors (剪刀)

    trousers (褲子)

Unit THREE

你能推薦一些商品給我嗎?

英文補給站 Track 2-4-03

Can you recommend something for me?
你能推薦一些商品給我嗎?

Can you show me something different?
還有其他不一樣的嗎?

How about this red shirt?
這件紅色T恤怎樣?

想要藉由逛街找到新穎潮貨(trendy)或是店內必買招牌(must),就要會問店員,Can you recommend something for me? (你能推薦一些商品給我嗎?)。

急用會話

CLERK Did you find anything you like?
你有找到你喜歡的東西了嗎?

JAMIE Can you recommend something for me?
你能推薦一些商品給我嗎?

CLERK How about this red shirt?
這件紅色T恤怎樣?

臨 時 用 語

1. 你喜歡那一件?:

Which one do you like?

2. 這就是你正在找的嗎?:

Is this what you are looking for?

3. 全部就這些嗎?:

Is that all?

Anything else?

Do you have anything thing better?

4. 這個顏色很流行:

This color is very popular.

This color is very smart.

This color is in fashion.

5. 這隻手鐲跟你的洋裝很配:

This bracelet goes well with your dress.

6. 這對耳環跟你很搭:

This pair of earrings fits you well.

Unit FOUR
這件衣服有大一號的嗎?

英文補給站

 Track 2-4-04

Do you have this in large?
這件衣服有大一號的嗎?
The fit isn't good.
尺寸不太合適。
Give me a smaller size, please.
請給我拿小一點的。

好不容易找到自己喜歡的東西,當然要先看一下是不適合自己,如果在試穿之前,就知道自己的尺寸,就可以直接跟服務人員要自己要的尺寸。記住不要說L, M, 或是S,一定要說完整的字(large, medium, small)。

急用會話

CLERK This black suit is stylish and in.
這件黑西裝正流行。
FRANK It's small. The fit isn't good.
這是小號的。尺寸不太合適。
Do you have this in a large?
這件衣服有大一號的嗎?

1. 什麼尺寸?:

What size?

2. 什麼顏色?:

What color?

3. 你穿多大號的鞋？:

What size shoes do you wear?

4. 可以給我大一號的嗎?:

Can I have a larger size?

5. 這件有36號的嗎?:

Do you have a size 36 in this?

6. 你們有這種鞋子嗎?:

Have you any shoes like these?

7. 你的尺寸已賣光了:

We are out of your size.

ᵁnit FIVE
我可以試穿嗎?

Track 2-4-05

Can I try this on?
我可以試穿嗎?

How is it?
如何?

It seems to fit you very well.
這件衣服很適合你。

找到你要的衣服,當然是要試穿看看囉。有些店裡會有fitting room(試衣間)的標示,如果一時之間找不到,我們可以直接跟店員說一聲,Can I try this on? (我可以試穿嗎?)。

急用會話

CATHERINE I like this one. May I try it on?
我喜歡這一種。我能試穿嗎?

CLERK Certainly. The fitting room is over there.
當然可以,試衣間在那邊。

CATHERINE How is it?
如何?

CLERK It fits you very well.
這件衣服很適合你。

1. 我能試穿嗎?:

Would you mind if I try this on?

I'd like to try this on.

Could I have a try?

2. 請試穿看看好嗎?:

Could you try it on please?

3. 你穿這個毛衣很合身:

That sweater looks very good on you.

That sweater goes well with you.

The sweater matches you well.

The sweater suits you well.

4. 太大了:

It's too big.

5. 太小了:

Too small.

Unit Six

你覺得這條項鍊如何?

Track 2-4-06

What do you think of this necklace?

你覺得這條項鍊如何?

How about this one?

這個如何呢?

I do not like this style.

我不喜歡這種樣式。

試穿戴上你找到的商品之後,你就可以問陪同你的親友或是店員,看起來如何 (How is it?)。如果不喜歡,我們可以說,I do not like this style. (我不喜歡這種樣式)。

PEONY What do you think of this necklace?

你覺得這條項鍊如何?

JOHN I do not like this style.

我不喜歡這種樣式。

CLERK How about this one?

這個如何呢?

PEONY Well, I will try it on.

好吧,我再試試看。

臨 時 用 語

1. 你覺得如何呢?:

What do you think of it?

What do you think?

How do you like it?

2. 你們有什麼樣式?:

What kind of style do you have?

3. 這是舊款嗎?:

Is it an old model?

4. 這些是新貨:

These are new arrivals.

5. 我不知道我的尺寸:

I don't know my size.

6. 可以幫我量一下尺寸嗎?:

Can you measure me up?

7. 這個顏色不是我的風格:

This color is not my style.

Unit SEVEN
商品還好嗎?

Track 2-4-07

Did you find everything all right?
商品還好嗎?

How did you find everything today?
商品還好嗎?

Everything is just fine.
還好。

通常在試衣間出來,店員會習慣性地問你Did you find everything all right? (商品還好嗎?),如果沒有太大的問題,你可以跟他說Everything is just fine. (還好)。或者是直接把你試穿的衣服還給他,並說Thank you.(謝謝)。如果你喜歡並要結帳購買,你可以跟他說,Yes, I will take it. (很好啊,我要這件)。

急用會話

CLERK Did you find everything all right?
商品還好嗎?

ZOE Everything is just fine.
還好。

Thank you.
謝謝。

臨 時 用 語

1. 我要這個：

I'll take this.

I will get this one.

2. 這尺寸不合：

It is not the right size.

3. 還有其他顏色嗎？：

Any other color?

4. 我這次先不買：

No. I will pass this time.

Not for this time.

I don't need any.

5. 我再看看：

I will browse around.

6. 慢慢來：

Take your time.

$\mathcal{Unit}$ Eight

這多少錢?

> How much does it cost?
> **這多少錢?**
> Can you make it cheaper?
> **你能便宜點嗎?**

看到喜歡的東西,要去結帳了,我們可以走到櫃台(desk),除了直接看商品標示牌(tag)付帳之外,也可以直接問店員,How much does it cost? (這多少錢?)

急用會話

NINA How much does it cost?
這多少錢?

CLERK It comes to two hundred and forty dollars.
總共240美元。

NINA Can you come down a little?
你能便宜點嗎?

CLERK That's the best I can do.
這是最合理的價格了。

288

臨 時 用 語

1. 我要付多少錢?:

How much do I have to pay for it?

What's the price of this one?

How much does it come to?

What's the price?

2. 這要100元:

It costs one hundred dollars.

It's priced at only one hundred dollars.

3. 你可以便宜一點嗎?:

Can you come down a bit?

Can you lower the price?

4. 你們有什麼特賣品嗎?:

Do you have anything on sale?

5. 這是我們的最低價了:

That's almost at cost.

That's our rock bottom price.

有打折嗎?

英文補給站

 Track 2-4-09

Is there any discount?

有打折嗎?

I have a membership card.

我有會員卡。

付錢時先想一想,自己身上有沒有membership card(會員卡),還是自己就是那間店的VIP(貴賓)。如果是,往往都會有打折(discount)的優惠服務。

急用會話

LILY Well, I have a membership card.

我有會員卡。

Is there any discount?

有打折嗎?

CLERK All right.

好吧。

I'll give it to you for 1000.

我算你一千元。

臨 時 用 語

1. 我是會員:

I am a member.

I am a VIP.

2. 那太貴了:

It costs too much.

It is too expensive.

We can't afford all that money.

3. 我有折價券:

I have a coupon.

4. 這有在拍賣嗎?:

Is it on sale?

5. 這不貴:

This is cheap.

This is inexpensive.

我可以用信用卡付款嗎?

 Track 2-4-10

Can I pay by credit card?

我可以用信用卡付款嗎?

Can I buy it on installments?

我可以分期付款嗎?

到了要付款的時候,我們可以詢問一下店內可使用的付款方式,然後選擇比較優惠的付款方法。

急用會話

PAULA Can I pay by credit card?

我可以用信用卡付款嗎?

CLERK Sure.

可以啊。

PAULA Can I buy it on installments?

我可以分期付款嗎?

CLERK Of course. You can pay a deposit of 100 dollars, and then 50 dollars a week for six months.

當然,你可以先付100元訂金,然後,每月付50元,一共付6個月。

臨 時 用 語

1. 我要如何付錢?:

How can I pay?

2. 我能開支票嗎?:

May I write a check for you?

Can I pay by check?

3. 你們接受旅行支票嗎?:

Do you take traveler's checks?

I would like to pay by traveler's check.

4. 對不起，我們不接受支票，請付現:

Sorry, we don't take checks. Please pay in cash.

單 字 解 說

1. check 名詞：支票
2. traveler's check 名詞：旅遊支票
3. cash 名詞：現金
4. credit card 名詞：信用卡

Unit ELEVEN
能不能把這些送到我家?

Do you have delivery service?
能不能把這些送到我家?
How long does it take before I get delivery?
要多久才能接到貨?

在外地購物或是網路購物(online shopping),付完款時,我們都可以選擇寄送貨物的服務。記得有需要時記得問店員一聲,Do you have delivery service? (能不能把這些送到我家?)。

急用會話

HELENA Do you have delivery services?
能不能把這些送到我家?
CLERK Sure. The delivery service is free.
有啊,宅配服務是免費的。
Please fill in this form and we will deliver your goods to the address.
請填這一個表格,然後我們就會把您的商品寄到這個地址。
HELENA Thank you.
謝謝。
CLERK With pleasure.

> 很榮幸為您服務。

臨 時 用 語

1. 你們送貨的服務嗎?:

Do you have pickup service?

2. 你們有退貨服務嗎?:

Do you offer refunds?

May I have a refund?

3. 你能換開20美元的錢嗎？:

Do you have change for a twenty-dollar bill?

4. 你們還進貨嗎?:

Are you likely to be getting any more in?

5. 你可以在你家附近的便利商店取貨:

You can pick up your product in a convenience store nearby your house.

6. 請跟客服部連絡:

Please contact customer service.

7. 對不起，我們沒有存貨了:

I'm sorry. It's out of stock.

I'm sorry. We haven't had any.

NOTE BOOK

國外旅行最急用 In Travelling

第五章

臨時
急用

用餐
Chapter Five Dining Out

𝕌𝕟𝕚𝕥 ONE
想不想出去吃?

 Track 2-5-01

Do you want to eat out?
想不想出去吃?

Do you like to eat out?
想不想出去吃?

Where do you want to eat today?
你今天想去哪裡吃?

外出旅行最令人雀躍的事情之一,就是計畫下一餐要吃什麼(What do you want to eat?)以及去哪裡吃 (Where do you want to eat?),讓旅程中充滿小小的驚喜。

急用會話

TIM Do you want to eat out?
想不想出去吃?

EMMA There is a deli across the street. Do you like it?
那裡有一家每日餐廳,你想去嗎?

TIM Sure. Let's go.
好啊,一起去吧!

298

1. 你可以推薦一下附近地一間餐廳嗎?:

Can you recommend a restaurant nearby?

2. 這附近有義式餐廳嗎?:

Is there any Italian restaurant around here?

3. 最近的中式餐廳在哪裡?:

Where is the nearest Chinese restaurant?

4. 我想找一間價位不貴的餐廳:

I want to go to an inexpensive restaurant.

I would like to go to a restaurant with reasonable prices.

5. 我想嘗試一下當地食物:

I'd like to try some local food.

6. 現在那裡還有餐廳是營業的嗎?:

Is any restaurant open now?

Unit TWO
我想預約四個人的座位

I would like to reserve a table for four.
我想預約四個人的座位。

We are a group of four.
我們共有四個人。

第一單元提到的Deli，比較是屬於街頭常間的小餐館，通常不需要預約。然而，國外一般規模大一些的餐廳，常常需要事先訂位(reserve a table)，不然就要在餐廳門前等上好一會兒囉。

急用會話

DELL Hello, I would like to reserve a table for four at six tonight.
嗨，我想預約今晚六點四個人的座位。

CLERK I'm sorry. We have so many guests this evening.
我很抱歉。今晚的客人相當多。

DELL How long is the wait?
我們大概需要等多久？

CLERK Eight o'clock should be O.K.
8點應該沒問題。

臨 時 用 語

1. 我需要預約位子嗎?:

Do I need a reservation?

2. 我要預約:

I want to make a reservation.

I would like to reserve a table.

(如果你要預約或預訂音樂會的票，我們會說
I want to book a ticket.。如果你是要跟人預約
工作上的會面，我們會說 I want to make an ap-
pointment.)

3. 我要如何才能到達餐廳?:

How can I get to the restaurant?

4. 我們需要等多久?:

How long do we have to wait for?

How long do we have to line up?

5. 餐廳是否有任何服裝上的規定?:

Any dress code?

我想要窗邊的座位

 Track 2-5-03

I would like a table by the window.
我想要窗邊的座位。

I prefer a table by the fireplace.
我喜歡靠壁爐的座位。

到了餐廳，常常會需要等人帶位，如果我們對
於座位有偏好的話，我們可以跟帶位者(usher)
說明。

急用會話

MARTIN Hello, I am Martin.
我是馬汀。

We have reserved a table for four.
我們已經預訂了四個人的座位。

USHER Sure. Please come with me.
好啊，跟我來。

MARTIN We would like a table by the
window.
我們想要窗邊的座位。

USHER Not a problem.
沒問題。

臨 時 用 語

1. 我想要坐在門邊:

I would like to sit by the door.

2. 我要坐在非吸菸區:

I would like to sit in the non-smoking area.

Non-smoking area, please.

(國外,尤其是歐洲地區,吸菸人口比較多。在帶位時,如果我們特別需要坐在非吸菸區時,一定要特別提醒帶位的人。)

3. 我要坐在吸菸區:

I want a smoking table.

I prefer a table in the smoking area.

(如果你本身就有吸菸的習慣,可以跟帶位者提醒,坐往吸菸區。)

4. 我要坐在安靜的角落:

I would like a quiet corner, please.

Unit FOUR
我們客滿了

How many in your party?
你們有幾位？

We are full.
我們客滿了。

We'll let you know as soon as a table is available.
有空位時，我們會馬上通知你。

如果沒有預約的話，在用餐時間，風景區的餐廳常常會呈現客滿狀態。這時候，我們就會聽見帶位者(usher)說，We are full. (我們客滿了)。

急用會話

USHER How many in your party?
你們有幾位？

PETER We are a group of four.
我們共有四個人。

USHER I am sorry, but we are full now.
我很抱歉，但是我們目前客滿。

We'll let you know as soon as a table is available.
有空位時，我們會馬上通知你。

臨 時 用 語

1. 我們現在客滿了，你們願意等嗎？：

We're full at the moment. Would you like to wait?

2. 我馬上回來：

I'll be with you in just a minute.

3. 對不起，我們六點才營業，現在還在準備中：

I'm sorry. We don't open until six o'clock. We're just getting set up now.

4. 要等半小時，這樣可以嗎？：

There is a half hour wait. Is that ok?

5. 抱歉讓你們久等了：

Sorry to keep you waiting.

6. 我們要關門了：

We are going to close.

7. 我們11點關門：

We will close at 11.

你可以點餐了嗎？

英文補給站

 Track 2-5-05

Are you ready to order?
你可以點餐了嗎？
What would you like?
你要吃些什麼？

坐上位子之後，就是準備點餐了。這個時候，
服務生(waiter)會給我們菜單(menu)，在我們
讀完之後，常會聽到服務生問一句，Are you
ready to order? (你可以點餐了嗎？)。

急用會話

WAITER Here is the menu.
這是菜單。
Are you ready to order?
你可以點餐了嗎？
YVONNE What do you have for today's
special?
今天的推薦餐是什麼？
WAITER Tomato soup.
番茄湯。

臨 時 用 語

1. 請給我菜單:

May I have a menu, please?

Menu, please.

2. 服務生!:

Waiter!

Waitress!

(waiter是用來稱呼男服務生,而waitress是用來
稱呼女服務生。)

3. 是否有中文菜單?:

Do you have a menu in Chinese?

4. 我可以點餐了嗎?:

May I order, please?

5. 決定好了再叫我:

Let me know when you're ready to
order.

6. 餐廳最特別的菜式是什麼?:

What is the specialty of the house?

Do you have today's special?

Unit SIX

你要喝點什麼嗎？

  Track 2-5-06

Would you like something to drink?

想喝些什麼嗎？

Any drinks?

喝些什麼嗎？

May I see the wine list?

可否讓我看看酒單？

在國外的較具規模的餐廳裡，什麼樣的餐點配上什麼樣的酒(drinks)，是很講究的。而且酒單(wine list)常常是額外付上的。所以，在點菜時，我們會聽到服務生特別問一句，Would you like something to drink? (想喝些什麼嗎？)。

急用會話

WAITER Would you like something to drink?

您要喝點什麼嗎？

VICTORIA A glass of white wine.

一杯白酒。

Thank you.

謝謝。

臨 時 用 語

1. 你們有什麼酒?：

What kind of drinks do you have?

What kind of wine do you have?

Anything to drink?

2. 我可以點杯酒嗎？：

May I order a glass of wine?

3. 是否可建議一些不錯的酒？：

Could you recommend some good wine?

4. 你們有酒精飲料嗎?：

Do you have alcoholic beverages?

Do you have some liquor?

Do you have drinks?

5. 常見酒類飲料(alcoholic beverage)英文：

wine 葡萄酒

red wine 紅葡萄酒

white wine 白葡萄酒

whiskey 威士忌

French wine 法國葡萄酒

champagne 香檳

beer 啤酒

cocktail 雞尾酒

gin 琴酒

rum 蘭姆酒

你們有無酒精飲料嗎？

英文補給站

 Track 2-5-07

Do you have non-alcoholic beverages?
你們有無酒精飲料嗎？
Soft drinks, please.
請給我無酒精飲料。

如果是開車，對酒精(alcohol)過敏，或是帶小孩同行，酒類飲料就不適合飲用了。這時候，我們在點餐時可以問服務生，Do you have non-alcoholic beverages? (你們有無酒精飲料嗎？)，並請他推薦。

急用會話

VICTOR Do you have non-alcoholic beverages?
你們有無酒精飲料嗎？
WAITER Yes. What would you like?
有啊，你要什麼？
VICTOR A cup of coffee, please.
請給我一杯咖啡。

臨 時 用 語

1. 你們有無酒精飲料嗎？：

Do you have any non-alcoholic
beverages?

2. 我對酒精過敏：

I am allergic to alcohol.

3. 一杯水就好了：

A glass of water will be fine.

(國外人士不太常喝熱開水，所以如果我們要喝
熱開水，一定要特別提醒，a glass of hot water,
please.)

4. 請給我一杯熱茶：

A cup of tea, please.

5. 常見無酒精飲料(beverages)英文：

tap water　自來水

lemonade　檸檬水

coco-cola(coke)　可口可樂

soda water　蘇打水

distilled water　蒸餾水

mineral water　礦泉水

black tea　紅茶

jasmine tea　茉莉(香片)

ginger ale　薑汁

orange juice　柳丁汁

juice　果汁

我要一杯拿鐵

英文補給站

 Track 2-5-08

A latte, please.
我要一杯拿鐵。
How would you like your latte?
你的拿鐵需要特別處理嗎?
Just regular.
一般就好。

咖啡(coffee)似乎已經是一種國際性的飲料。無論去到哪,都可以看到咖啡店(caf)的蹤影。用英文點一杯我們自己喜歡的咖啡,也成為出國旅行中,令人欣喜的一件事情了。

急用會話

JANET A latte, please.
我要一杯拿鐵。
CLERK How would you like your latte?
你的拿鐵需要特別處理嗎?
JANET Just regular.
一般就好。

臨 時 用 語

1. 你要加冰嗎?:
Would you like ice?

2. 你可以幫我加糖嗎?:
Could you add some sugar for me?

3. 可以少糖嗎?:
Less sugar, please.

4. 我的咖啡無糖去冰:
I want my coffee with no ice and no sugar.

5. 常見咖啡英文用語:

Espresso 義式濃縮咖啡

Americano 美式咖啡

Cappuccino 卡布奇諾

Latte 牛奶咖啡

Mocha 摩卡

Macchiato 瑪奇雅朵咖啡

Decaf 低咖啡因咖啡

drip coffee 滲漏式咖啡

instant coffee 即溶咖啡

cream 奶油

milk 牛奶

caffeine 咖啡因

Unit NINE
請給我一些甜點

 Track 2-5-09

I would like some dessert, please.
請給我一些甜點。

What do you have for dessert?
甜點有那幾種?

May I have some bread, please?
請給我一些麵包。

一般餐廳的餐點基本上大致會分成前菜(entree)、沙拉(salad)、湯(soup)、主食(main course)、甜點(dessert)、飲料(beverages)等大項。我們在點餐或用餐時,就可以說I would like some _____, please. (請給我一些 _____)。

急用會話

WAITER May I take your order, please?
我可以幫您點餐了嗎?

CINDY Sure. May I have some bread, please?
請給我一些麵包。

Also, I would like some dessert, please.
也請給我一些甜點。

1. 可以給我一點這個嗎？：
May I have just a little of it?

2. 可不可以不要甜點改要水果？：
Can I have some fruit instead of the dessert?

3. 有咖啡做為附餐嗎？：
Is coffee included in this meal?

4. 你要什麼甜點？：
What would you like for dessert?

5. 我要霜淇淋：
I'll have some ice cream.

6. 你要水果嗎？：
Do you want some fruit?

7. 你的菜來了：
Here is your food.

我正在節食中

英文補給站

 Track 2-5-10

I'm on a diet.

我正在節食中。

I am a vegetarian.

我是素食者。

May I smoke?

可以抽煙嗎？

到餐廳用餐，如果有個人需求，我們可以在點餐中跟服務生一一說明，請求協助。本單元介紹各種常見的點餐需求。

急用會話

VIVIAN I'm on a diet.

我正在節食中。

I cannot take much fat and sugar.

我不能攝取太多油脂跟糖分。

WAITER I see. I will make a note of it for you.

我知道了，我會記下來。

臨 時 用 語

1. **餐廳是否有供應素食餐？：**

Do you have any vegetarian dishes?

2. **我不吃乳製品：**

No dairy products, please.

I do not eat any dairy products.

3. **我不能吃太多鹽：**

I cannot take too much salt.

4. **我對海產過敏：**

I am allergic to seafood.

5. **我不能吃蔥蒜：**

I cannot have onion or garlic.

6. **請告訴我要如何食用這道菜？：**

Could you tell me how to eat this?

7. **請把鹽/胡椒傳給我：**

Could you pass me the salt/pepper?

Unit ELEVEN
這真好吃

Yummy!

這真好吃！

It is delicious.

這真好吃！

Yuck.

這不好吃。

去餐廳吃東西，朋友之間會討論到食物是否好吃。如果好吃，我們可以說Yummy或是Delicious。如果不好吃，我們除了可以默不作聲表示禮貌之外，也可以說Yuck。

急用會話

WILLIAM This restaurant is famous for its steak.

這間餐廳以它的牛排有名。

KATE Hum… it is really delicious.

這真的很好吃耶。

WILLIAM I've told you already.

我早就說了吧。

臨 時 用 語

1. 這真好吃：

It is tasty.

It is good.

2. 這沒有味道：

It is tasteless.

3. 這很噁心：

It is disgusting.

4. 這沒有熟：

It is not cooked all the way through.

The meat is not done.

5. 我點的食物還沒來：

My order hasn't come yet.

6. 這不是我點的食物：

This is not what I ordered.

Unit TWELVE

你要牛排幾分熟?

英文補給站

 Track 2-5-12

> How do you like your steak?
>
> **你要牛排幾分熟?**
>
> How do you like your eggs?
>
> **你的蛋要幾分熟?**

去到餐廳,常常會聽到服務生問你說,How do you like＿＿＿? (你要你的＿＿＿怎麼處理?)。牛排跟蛋是最常被詢問的餐點,所以本單元將介紹點牛排跟蛋的說法。

急用會話

WAITER How do you like your steak?

你要牛排幾分熟?

GREG I want it medium.

我要五分熟。

WAITER How do you like your eggs?

你的蛋要幾分熟?

GREG Sunny-side up.

只煎一面就好了。

臨 時 用 語

1. 牛排料理英文說法:

全熟: well done

七分熟: medium well

五分熟: medium

四分熟: medium rare

三分熟: rare

2. 蛋的料理說法:

炒蛋: scrambled

荷包蛋(只煎一面): sunny side up

荷包蛋(兩面都煎): over easy

白煮蛋(蛋黃液狀): soft boiled

白煮蛋(蛋黃固狀): hard boiled

3. 還要我為你做什麼嗎?:

What else can I help you with?

4. 這燒焦了吧!:

Did you burn it?

Did you burn something?

5. 你吃完了嗎?:

Have you finished?

Unit THIRTEEN
麻煩請結帳

英文補給站

 Track 2-5-13

Check, please.
麻煩請結帳。

Bring me the bill please.
請買單。

Can I pay with this credit card?
可以用這張信用卡付帳嗎？

吃飽喝足了，就是準備要結帳的時候。要結
帳時，除了可以用手勢(gesture)或是眼神(eye
contact)示意服務生結帳，或是我們可以說，
Check, please.(麻煩請結帳)。

急用會話

WAITER Have you finished?
你吃完了嗎？

PENNY Yes, and I am full.
是啊，而且我吃得飽。

Check, please.
麻煩請結帳。

1. 可以在這兒付帳嗎？：
Can I pay here?

2. 我能用支票或信用卡嗎？：
Can I pay by chcck or credit card?

3. 我們想要分開算帳：
We'd like to pay separately.

4. 找您的錢：
Here is your change.

5. 我請客：
It is on me.
It is my treat.
Let me foot the bill.

6. 我吃飽了：
I am up to my ears.
I am stuffed.

NOTE BOOK

Ladies and gentlemen, welcome to our hotel, where yo
Do you need any help?
I need some vegetables and
Many students like to stay at hom
How about coming with u
It is a coincidence that my bir

國外旅行最急用 In Travelling

第六章

機場

Chapter Six In the Airport

e veget
students like to stay at hou
oming with us?
that my birthday is the same as hers,

Unit ONE
我要訂機位

Track 2-6-01

I would like to book a ticket to Tokyo.
我要訂一張去東京的機票。
One ticket to New York, please.
一張去紐約的機票。

出國旅行，機場(airport)是我們必經之地，如果是自助旅行，熟悉機場英文會話，更是讓我們所向無敵的王道。這個單元，我們將從訂機票(book a flight ticket)開始，Let's go。

急用會話

SALES REPRESENTATIVE May I help you?
有什麼是我可以為您效勞的?
JACK I would like to book a ticket to Tokyo.
我要訂一張去東京的機票。
SALES REPRESENTATIVE No problem. We have one flight to Tokyo at 12 p.m.
沒問題。我們中午十二點有一架班機飛往東京。
JACK That would be fine.
好的。

臨 時 用 語

1. 我想訂一張巴黎台北來回票:

I would like to book a round-trip ticket from Taipei to Paris.

I would like to make a reservation for a round-trip flight from Taipei to Paris.

2. 你想要訂哪一種艙等:

How would you like to fly?

3. 還有機位嗎?:

Is there any seat available?

4. 飛機何時起飛?

What time will the flight take off?

What time will the flight depart?

When is the departure time?

單 字 解 說

機票英文常見單詞:

單程票: one-way ticket

來回票: round-trip ticket

回程時間未定的票: open return

頭等艙: first class

商務艙: business class

經濟艙: economy class

Unit TWO
我要報到登機

英文補給站

 Track 2-6-02

I would like to check in.
我要報到登機。
May I have your passport and ticket?
可以給我你的護照跟機票嗎?

一般國際線除了要在起飛時間前三小時到機場
報到登機(check-in),記得在找到報到櫃台後,
跟服務人員說一聲,I would like to check in. (我
要報到登機)。

急用會話

LEE I would like to check in.
我要報到登機。
GROUND STAFF Sure. May I have your
passport and ticket?
可以給我你的護照跟機票嗎?
LEE Here you are.
在這裡。
GROUND STAFF Would you like a window
or an aisle seat?
您要靠窗的座位還是走道的座位?
LEE A window seat, please.
靠窗的。

臨 時 用 語

1. 你想要什麼座位?:

Do you have any seating preference?

Where would you like to sit?

2. 我要靠走道/靠窗/中間坐位:

I would like an aisle/ a window/ a

middle seat.

3. 你有行李嗎?:

Do you have any luggage?

Do you need to check in any luggage?

Do you have any luggage to check in?

4. 我有兩件行李/托運行李/手提行李:

I have two suitcases/check-in bags/

carry-on bags.

5. 請將行李放在磅秤上:

Please put your suitcase on the scale.

6. 行李過重:

The luggage is overweight.

The luggage is over the limit.

Unit THREE
請問轉機應該怎麼走？

Can you tell me where to transfer, please?

請問轉機應該怎麼走？

Where is Terminal 3?

第三航廈怎麼走？

在機場裡，找航廈(terminal)或是行程時刻表(time table)，確認航班(flight)，都是讓我們行程更順暢的過程。本單元介紹機場問路英文句子，平時多練習，需要用的時候，別忘大聲地問一句，Where is＿＿＿?(＿＿＿在哪裡?)。

TIM Can you tell me where to transfer, please?

請問轉機應該怎麼走？

CLERK Do you have the boarding pass for the next flight?

您有下個航班的登機證嗎？

Well, you should go to the Terminal 3.

你應該往第三航廈去。

TIM Where is Terminal 3?

第三航廈怎麼走？

330

CLERK Follow the sign and take the shuttle bus.

沿著指標，然後搭接駁車吧。

臨 時 用 語

1. **我要怎麼去第十登機門?:**

Where is Gate 10?

How do I get to Gate 10 from here?

2. **什麼時候登機?:**

When is the boarding time?

3. **飛機準時起飛:**

The flight should take off on time.

4. **這是你的登機卡:**

Here's your boarding pass.

5. **祝你旅途愉快:**

Have a nice flight.

單 字 解 說

機場常見標示英文說法:

出境: departure

入境: arrival

海關: customs

劃位櫃台: check-in counter

班機班次表: flight timetable

免稅商店: duty-free shop

Unit FOUR

你能幫我放行李嗎?

英文補給站

 Track 2-6-04

Can you help me with the luggage?
你能幫我放行李嗎?
Down this aisle, to your left.
走道直走,座位在左手邊。

到了機艙(cabin),空服員(flight attendant)會協助我們找到座位(seat)。在飛機上,如果我們需要協助,只要記得開口說,空服員們也會親切地提供。

急用會話

FLIGHT ATTENDANT Welcome abroad.
歡迎登機。
SHELDON Where is my seat?
我的座位在哪兒呢?
FLIGHT ATTENDANT Down this aisle, to your left.
走道直走,座位在左手邊。
SHELDON Can you help me with the luggage?
你能幫我放行李嗎?
FLIGHT ATTENDANT Sure.
好啊。

臨 時 用 語

1. 請給我你的背包：

Please give me your backpacks.

2. 我把背包放在頭上的置物櫃：

I will put the backpacks in the overhead
compartment.

3. 有報紙嗎?：

Do you have any newspapers?

4. 有中文報紙嗎?：

Do you have any newspapers in
Chinese?

May I have a Chinese newspaper,
please?

5. 請坐好並繫上安全帶：

Please sit down and buckle up.

6. 禁止吸菸：

No smoking here.

7. 請關機：

Please turn off your cell phone.

𝔘nit FIVE
你要吃什麼呢?

英文補給站

 Track 2-6-05

What would you like?
你要吃什麼呢?
Coffee, tea, or juice?
咖啡,茶,或是果汁?

坐飛機其中一件令人興奮的事就是飛機上的餐點(meal)了。通常我們可以在坐飛機時就先讀過菜單(menu),先想好自己要吃什麼。在送餐時,空服員會問我們的需求,此時記得大膽地把平日練習好的英文說出來,為自己點一份滿意的飛機餐(airplane food)。

急用會話

FLIGHT ATTENDANT What would you like?
你要吃什麼呢?
HELEN Chicken, please.
雞肉好了。
FLIGHT ATTENDANT Coffee, tea, or juice?
咖啡,茶,或是果汁?
HELEN Coffee, please.
咖啡吧。

臨 時 用 語

1. 你早餐/午餐/晚餐想吃什麼?:

What would you like for breakfast/
lunch/ dinner?

2. 我想要一杯水:

I would like to have a glass of water.

3. 我還想要一些麵包:

May I have some more bread?

4. 要喝什麼嗎?:

Anything to drink?

5. 請給我紅酒:

Please give me a glass of wine.

6. 我馬上回來:

I will be right with you.

I will be right over.

Coming right up.

𝒰nit SIX

請問洗手間怎麼走?

英文補給站

 Track 2-6-06

> Can you show me where the lavatory is?
> 請問洗手間怎麼走?
>
> Can you take me to the lavatory?
> 請問洗手間怎麼走?
>
> Please give me a deck of cards.
> 請給我撲克牌。

在漫漫的飛行中,我們常會需要空服員的服務。有任何需要時,除了按服務燈(press the service button)等候空服員,更別忘了用英文說出自己的需求。本單元將介紹在飛航時一般常見的服務需求。

急用會話

LINDA Can you show me where the lavatory is?
請問洗手間怎麼走?

FLIGHT ATTENDANT Down the aisle to your right.
走道底,在右手邊。

LINDA Please give me a deck of cards.
請給我撲克牌。

> **FLIGHT ATTENDANT** Yes. I will be right with you.
> 好的。我馬上回來。

臨 時 用 語

1. 我要購買免稅商品：

May I purchase duty-free goods?

2. 可以教我怎麼把餐盤放下嗎？：

Could you show me how to put the tray table down?

3. 可以教我怎麼把座椅直立嗎？：

Could you show me how to put my seat upright?

4. 可以教我怎麼把窗簾關上嗎？：

Could you show me how to pull down the window shade?

5. 我可以再要一副耳機嗎？：

May I have another pair of headphones?

6. 我要毯子：

May I have a blanket, please?

7. 有會說中文的空服員嗎？：

Is there a flight attendant on board who can speak Chinese?

𝒰nit SEVEN
我們來這裡觀光

  Track 2-6-07

> What's the purpose of your visit?
> **旅行的目的為何?**
> We are here for sightseeing.
> **我們來觀光。**

飛機降落,入境之後,海關人員會詢問我們來到這個國家的目的。這個時候,英文一定要練好,好跟海關人員說明,我們此趟行程的目的是為了移民(for immigration)、為了觀光(for sightseeing)、還是為了商務(on business)。

急用會話

IMMIGRATION OFFICER May I see your passport, please?
請給我你的護照。
EMMA Sure. Here you are.
好啊,在這。
IMMIGRATION OFFICER What's the purpose of your visit?
你此行的目的為何?
EMMA We are here for sightseeing.
我們來觀光。

臨 時 用 語

1. 你此行的目的為何?:

What's your reason for visiting here?

What brings you here?

2. 這是我的護照:

Here is my passport.

Here it is.

3. 你會住哪?:

Where will you stay?

4. 你預計待多久?:

How long do you plan to stay?

5. 你自己一個人來旅行嗎?:

Are you travelling alone?

單 字 解 說

表示旅行目的常見英文說法:

觀光: sightseeing / touring

商旅: business

移民: immigration

拜訪親友: visiting friends and relatives

參加會議: attending a conference /
meeting / seminar

你有東西要申報的嗎?

英文補給站

 Track 2-6-08

Do you have anything to declare?

你有東西要申報的嗎?

How much money do you have with you?

你隨身攜帶多少現金?

過海關時,海關人員除了會問我們此行的目的之外,也會問我們有沒有東西要申報(Do you have anything to declare?)。如果我們攜帶的現金金額超過規定,或是攜帶了貴重珠寶,一定要記得填申報表(customs declaration form)申報。

急用會話

CUSTOMS OFFICER Do you have anything to declare?

你有東西要申報的嗎?

PETER I have nothing to declare.

我沒有東西要申報。

CUSTOMS OFFICER How much money do you have on you?

你隨身攜帶多少現金?

PETER I have one hundred US dollars.

我帶了一百元美金。

臨 時 用 語

1. 你行李箱裝了什麼?:

What do you have in this suitcase?

2. 你有帶禮物或是貴重物品嗎?:

Don't you have any gifts or valuable
articles?

3. 你有帶香菸或酒嗎?:

Do you have any cigarettes or liquor?

4. 這些是我私人使用的東西:

These are for my personal use.

5. 這些是紀念品:

These are souvenirs.

6. 這是給朋友的禮物:

These are gifts for friends.

7. 祝你玩得愉快:

Have a nice day.

Have a nice stay.

Unit NINE
我的行李不見了

I can't find my baggage.
我的行李不見了。
Where is the lost luggage office?
行李遺失申報處在哪？

出境之後，最重要的事就是領行李(claim the luggage)了。一般來說，通常我們到了行李提領區(baggage claim area)，都可以領到我們的行李。萬一行李遺失，記得趕快跟工作人員說一聲，I can't find my baggage.(我的行李不見了)。

急用會話

NADIA Excuse me, I can't find my baggage.
不好意思，我的行李不見了。
Where is the lost luggage office?
行李遺失申報處在哪？
OFFICER Please come with me to the office.
請和我到辦公室？

臨 時 用 語

1. 行李提領區怎麼走?:

Where is the baggage claim area?

Where is the baggage service?

2. 我可以在哪裡領行李?:

Where can I get my baggage?

3. 我可以在哪找到行李推車？:

Where can I get a luggage cart?

4. 這是我的行李托運卡:

Here is my baggage claim tag.

5. 我的行李不見了:

My baggage is missing.

I want to report a lost bag.

6. 我的行李損壞了:

My baggage is damaged.

7. 請你一找到行李便立即送到我住的飯
   店:

Please deliver my baggage to my hotel
as soon as you find it.

從零開始學韓語單字

收錄初學者必背的單字
同時也是韓檢初級最常考的生字
針對每個詞彙
補充類義詞、反義詞、相關詞彙,
以及好用的例句
更詳細整理出動詞、形容詞的基本變化
小小一本,讓你輕鬆帶著走

就是這一本超實用韓語單字書

初學者必會的基礎單字
生活上常用的單字會話一應俱全
小小一本,韓語單字立即上手

就是這一本超實用的旅遊英語

專為初學者設計
提供最實用的英語會話句子
一次搞定英語旅遊會話！
旅行不能忘記帶的英文小寶典！

從零開始學韓語會話

收錄初學者必學的韓語會話
本書依據各種話題，同時整理出會話、
文法、單字，以及補充例句，
讓初學者的你不小心就學會韓語，
從此想和韓國人聊天不再有口難言！

輕鬆學韓語：生活實用篇

想要一次學好韓語單字、會話及文法嗎？
這本韓語學習書囊括了所有生活中會出現
的單字、會話以及例句。同時針對基本動
詞、句型做最詳盡的解說，就算你是初學
者，也能自信滿滿地開口說韓語！

韓檢TOPIK初級中級單字一本就夠

本書整理出TOPIK韓語檢定考試必出的
初、中級詞彙，針對動詞、形容詞舉出
相關例句幫助學習，同時歸納出考生最
容易搞混、出錯的動詞以及形容詞變化
配合朗讀MP3加強聽力讓您輕輕鬆鬆取
得韓語初、中級證照！

永續圖書
線上購物網

www.foreverbooks.com.tw

◆ 加入會員即享活動及會員折扣。

◆ 每月均有優惠活動，期期不同。

◆ 新加入會員三天內訂購書籍不限本數金額，

　即贈送精選書籍一本。（依網站標示為主）

專業圖書發行、書局經銷、圖書出版

永續圖書總代理：

五觀藝術出版社、培育文化、棋茵出版社、達觀出版社、

可道書坊、白橡文化、大拓文化、讀品文化、雅典文化、

知音人文化、手藝家出版社、璞珅文化、智學堂文化、語

言鳥文化

活動期內，永續圖書將保留變更或終止該活動之權利及最終決定權。

英語館 系列 06

臨時急用！
你一定會用到的生活英語會話

 編著　臧琪蕾　 執行編輯　許純華　 美術編輯　翁敏貴

出版社

22103　新北市汐止區大同路三段１８８號９樓之１
TEL　（02）8647-3663
FAX　（02）8647-3660

法律顧問　方圓法律事務所　涂成樞律師

總經銷：永續圖書有限公司
永續圖書線上購物網
www.foreverbooks.com.tw

CVS代理　美璟文化有限公司
　　　　　TEL　（02）2723-9968
　　　　　FAX　（02）2723-9668
出版日　2013年01月

國家圖書館出版品預行編目資料

臨時急用!你一定會用到的生活英語會話 / 臧琪蕾編著.
　-- 初版. -- 新北市：語言鳥文化, 民102.01
　　　面；　公分. --（英語館；6）
　　ISBN 978-986-88955-1-5(平裝附光碟片)

　1. 英語 2. 會話

805. 188　　　　　　　　　　　　　　101022650

語言鳥 Parrot 讀者回函卡

臨時急用！
你一定會用到的生活英語會話

感謝您對這本書的支持，請務必留下您的基本資料及常用的電子信箱，以傳真、掃描或使用我們準備的免郵回函寄回。我們每月將抽出一百名回函讀者寄出精美禮物，並享有生日當月購書優惠價，語言鳥文化再一次感謝您的支持與愛護！

想知道更多即時的消息，歡迎加入"永續圖書粉絲團"

傳真電話：　　　　　　　　　　　電子信箱：
（02）8647-3660　　　　　　　　yungjiuh@ms45.hinet.net

基本資料

姓名：＿＿＿＿＿　○先生　　電話：＿＿＿＿＿
　　　　　　　　 ○小姐

E-mail：＿＿＿＿＿

地址：＿＿＿＿＿

購買此書的縣市及地點：＿＿＿＿＿

□連鎖書店　□一般書局　□量販店　□超商

□書展　□郵購　□網路訂購　□其他＿＿＿＿＿

您對於本書的意見

內容	：	□滿意	□尚可	□待改進
編排	：	□滿意	□尚可	□待改進
文字閱讀	：	□滿意	□尚可	□待改進
封面設計	：	□滿意	□尚可	□待改進
印刷品質	：	□滿意	□尚可	□待改進

您對於敝公司的建議

新北市汐止區大同路三段188號9樓之1

語言鳥文化事業有限公司

編輯部　收

請沿此虛線對折免貼郵票，以膠帶黏貼後寄回，謝謝！

語言是通往世界的橋梁